CONFLICT IN LITTLE LEAF CREEK

A LITTLE LEAF CREEK COZY MYSTERY

CINDY BELL

CONTENTS

eady eyes, and thick, long teeth inched closer to her.

Cassie Alberta bit down into her bottom lip and wondered what would be the best thing to do. Should she stay perfectly still? Make a run for it? She glanced toward the gate in the chain link fence. Too far.

A high-pitched grunt drew her attention back to the determined stares of her two captors. If only she hadn't brought them a gift, they might not have cornered her in her neighbor's yard.

"Easy boys." Cassie held out her hands as the goats crept closer to her.

As she tried to back away faster, they matched her pace. There was no way she could outrun them.

"I know, I know, I brought this on myself." Cassie drew a sharp breath, then shook her head as a burst of panic threatened to overtake her. "But I had no idea that you would be so fond of the carrots from my garden. If you just give me a moment, I can get more."

Her fingertips danced perilously along the sharp edges of the top of the chain link fence behind her, in search of the gate that would allow her to escape the yard, and the two very hungry goats.

The back door of the house that the chain link fence surrounded swung open with a bang.

"Shoo there!" A shrill but rough voice called out. "Leave her be, you greedy goats!"

A dog burst past the door, and the woman who held it open, then sailed over the two steps attached to the back porch, and landed right between the two goats.

Instantly, the two goats skittered off in opposite directions, around either side of the house, toward the front of the property. Barks and bleats filled the air as the dog continued to chase the goats. Cassie had never been so happy to see Harry, the collie mix.

A sigh of relief burst past Cassie's lips, followed by an embarrassed laugh as she looked up at the woman still on the back porch.

"Thanks, Tessa, you saved me!"

"Let me guess, you were trying to spoil them with treats again?" Tessa Watters, a woman in her sixties, walked down the steps into the yard. She walked toward Cassie with an uneven gait. Her silver hair framed her face in short, layered waves. Her striking blue eyes settled on Cassie with certainty. "Haven't I warned you about that?"

"Yes, you have." Cassie's shoulders slumped as her laughter faded. The woman who walked toward her was twenty years her senior and she felt dwarfed by her wisdom and confidence. "And, I didn't listen. I really didn't think they would like carrots so much. I thought, if I bribed them with a few they might like me a little better."

"They're goats." Tessa shrugged as a smile cracked her stern expression. "They'll eat anything you give them, but they won't stop being ornery. That's why we get along so well. We understand each other."

"I promise, I won't try to bribe them anymore." Cassie smiled in return, warmed by the presence of the friend she'd made since moving to the small town of Little Leaf Creek. It had been a big change from the glitz and demands of the city, where she'd spent twenty years of her life as a CEO's socialite wife. She had been the manager at a small museum, but her first priority was being a CEO's wife. Now, in dusty jeans, her heart still racing from her close encounter with two determined goats, she was still adjusting to her new lifestyle.

"Oh, don't disappoint them." Tessa shook her head as she crossed her arms over her stomach and grinned. "Then they'll really hate you."

"Great, I'm in a bit of a mess, aren't I?" Cassie rolled her eyes as she resisted the urge to hug Tessa. Although the gruff woman had warmed up to her to some degree, she was quite certain that hugs were still off the table.

"I've got some coffee ready, come on in." Tessa turned and started up the steps toward the kitchen door. "Get it while it's hot."

Cassie eagerly followed after her. At least in the house, for the moment, she'd be safe from the goats. Tessa adored her pets. Harry followed close behind them. Cassie felt lucky to be invited into her home, since for the most part, Tessa kept completely to herself, and preferred the outside world, remain outside.

"It smells so delicious in here!" Cassie sucked in a deep breath of blueberry laced air and sighed as she poured herself a cup of fresh coffee.

"Just made these muffins." Tessa gestured to the platter on the counter. "I was in the mood for baking."

"I'm so glad you were." Cassie grinned as she plucked one of the muffins off of the platter. For all of Tessa's toughness, when it came to baking, another side of her surfaced. Cassie had witnessed it a few times. As she stirred ingredients together, or tasted the batter in search of what might be missing, her muscles relaxed, her voice softened, the hardness in her expression faded into something almost whimsical. The moments were elusive, and impossible to pin down, but when she spotted one, Cassie tried to take a mental picture of it.

"With the holiday coming up, I think everyone's getting the baking bug." Cassie sat down in one of the retro-style metal chairs and set her coffee and muffin on the kitchen table. "I'm looking forward to trying out a few new recipes."

"Holiday?" Tessa carried her own muffin and coffee to the table and sat in the only other chair. Tessa's home wasn't set up to support very many guests. Even her living room only had two easy chairs and a television, with nothing that invited anyone to stay longer than they had to.

"Thanksgiving." Cassie met her eyes, then took a

nibble of the muffin. "Oh, so good. How do you make everything perfect every time?"

"Perfect." Tessa gave a short laugh. "I suppose you've sampled enough blueberry muffins in your lifetime to know what makes one perfect?"

"All I know is that whatever you make melts in my mouth." Cassie closed her eyes as she savored another bite. "This is definitely the highlight of my day."

"I think you've been alone in that house too long." Tessa shook her head, then sipped her coffee.

"I guess we both have been." Cassie peeked over the top of her coffee mug. "So maybe we could be alone, together, on Thanksgiving? I'd love to have you over. The house is finally coming together and I'm sure that you would enjoy it." She took a breath, prepared to launch into more convincing chatter, but before she could Tessa set her mug down hard on the table.

"No."

"No?"

"Not a chance. It's not going to happen, Cassie. Drop it."

"Tessa."

Tessa took a loud slurp of her coffee.

"We don't even have to call it Thanksgiving, we

can just call it a get together." Cassie toyed with the handle of her mug and forced as much cheer into her voice as she could summon.

"Cassie, are we friends?" Tessa's eyes locked to hers, their cool blue shade carrying an icy chill.

Cassie's chest tightened, capturing a breath between her throat and her lungs, as she braced herself for the consequences her answer might bring.

"I hope we are."

"I do, too." A smile flickered across Tessa's lips. "So, drop it."

Cassie offered a light nod and focused on her muffin. Occasionally, as Tessa baked, and they chatted about the town of Little Leaf Creek, or the behavior of mischievous goats, Cassie forgot that Tessa was an intimidating woman. But a moment, not unlike the current one, always surfaced to remind her of the truth. Yes, she hoped they were friends, but she also knew that friendship was stretched as taut as a tightrope, ready to snap with the wrong move.

"Thanks." Cassie stood up from the table, the tension between them still thick as she turned toward the door.

"Cassie wait." Tessa's voice softened as she stood up as well.

"Yes?" Cassie turned back toward her, eager to hear what she had to say.

"Here, take these." Tessa gave the curve of her hip a hard slap. "I definitely don't need to eat the whole batch myself, and you could certainly use some rounding."

Cassie smiled as she took the muffins from Tessa. She knew the other woman was only teasing. Cassie had certainly had more than her share of sweet treats since she had moved to Little Leaf Creek.

"Thanks Tessa. Are you sure about Thanksgiving? We still have plenty of time to plan, and I'd love to try out some recipes."

"I'm quite sure." Tessa locked her eyes to Cassie's and lifted one eyebrow just far enough to sharpen her stare.

"Okay, I hear you." Cassie forced a smile, then hurried back out through the door.

Cassie was almost to the gate between Tessa and her house, when she heard the pounding of two goats headed straight for her. "Stop, Billy, Gerry!" She shrieked and threw a muffin in their direction as she ducked through the gate. She slammed it closed behind her as the two goats shoved at each other to get the larger share of the muffin.

Amused, Cassie watched them for a moment, before the sound of a rumbling engine drew her attention to the street in front of her house. Early morning sunshine reflected off of the sculpture displayed in the center of her yard, created by a local, young artist. It was the first purchase she made in Little Leaf Creek, after buying her home. As her attention shifted back to the blue pickup truck, its driver stepped out. Sebastian Vail.

Cassie paused a moment and observed the way he tugged his cap down lower over his straight, blond hair, shielding his sun-tanned face from the sun's insistent rays. His focus remained on gathering some supplies from the back of his truck, but abruptly, he looked up at her, too fast for her to look away and pretend she wasn't staring. She set the tray of muffins down on the table on the front porch, then hurried toward him.

"Morning Sebastian, hi," Cassie stumbled over her words as she walked toward him. "Let me help you with that."

"Sure, if you want to grab a few paint cans." Sebastian tipped his head in the direction of several cans of paint lined up in the back of the truck. "I don't think we'll use them all today, but there was a sale."

"Great." Cassie grabbed two of the cans which were surprisingly heavy as they hung from her hands. "Thanks again for doing this."

"It's my pleasure." Sebastian winked at her from beneath the rim of his baseball cap. "I live to serve the ladies of Little Leaf Creek."

Cassie resisted rolling her eyes. She knew he

meant his comment to be teasing, but he wasn't far off the mark. Most of the single women in Little Leaf Creek were in quite a heated competition to catch the eye of the jack-of-all-trades that charmed them with his smooth accent and his warm, dark brown eyes. Not her of course. At least, that's what she'd been trying to convince herself of, since the last time he'd stared so hard into her eyes that her heart stopped beating for just a second. He had his choice of women, not to mention the fact that he was two years younger than her.

"Coming through." Sebastian carried a ladder between her and the front gate of the house, then propped it up against the front porch. "I think we'll be able to get a good first coat going today. I sanded all of the troublesome patches yesterday, so we should be in good shape."

"Wonderful, I'm curious about how it will look." Cassie gazed at the dingy exterior of the house she'd claimed as her own. A paint job wasn't the only thing it needed, but it was a good place to start. The two-story structure was a far cry from the penthouse style apartment she'd shared with her late husband. What it lacked in luxury, it made up for in nostalgia, as it was quite similar to the house she'd grown up in. Her life had started out in a town, just about as small as Little Leaf Creek, and the draw of that simple life had inspired her to try to find it again. Something slower, quieter. Something that could soothe the wounds that a loveless marriage and a life of trying to fit into high society had created.

"Morning Cassie." A car stopped just outside the fence, right behind Sebastian's blue pickup truck. The dark-haired man behind the wheel leaned his head out through the window and settled his gray gaze on her. "Hard at work already?"

"Just getting started." Cassie turned with a smile to face Detective Oliver Graham. He was one of the first people she'd encountered in Little Leaf Creek, and although his demeanor left a lot to be desired, she sensed that his heart was in the right place.

As Cassie looked at him she recalled when they had last seen each other. They had planned to go on a date a few weeks ago, but it got cancelled due to the pursuit of a murderer. She'd been convinced that it was too soon to even consider dating, but against her better judgement she had decided to go to dinner with him. Eventually, they rescheduled their date.

Cassie had become quite well acquainted with Little Leaf Creek's police detective. He was highly focused on his work. His attention to detail was something that she very much admired, and yet it might have been what unraveled their first date. Their dinner had been a disaster. She could recall her attempts to choose a meal, how nervous she felt, the flutter in her heart when he looked at her, and the tension in her muscles when he placed his hand over hers.

Cassie guessed that he had noticed, too. He seemed so nervous that they'd barely been able to get a conversation going, and once they did, it had ended in a mild but frustrating argument about following the rules.

At the end of the evening, Oliver had said that he enjoyed her company but he didn't want to lose the friendship they had and he thought they should just remain friends. The way he had looked at her when he said it left her unsettled. He was too hard for her to read. She had been right. The date hadn't gone well.

Cassie was relieved, as although she could see them being friends, her husband had passed away less than a year ago, and she wasn't sure if she was ready for a relationship. She also didn't want to string him along and then hurt him, as he seemed to take everything so seriously.

That was that then. They were just friends. So,

why did it feel so strange to her that things had ended that way? She pushed the thought from her mind. She had many adventures ahead of her. She just had to find a way to keep her mind open to them all. At least Oliver had been brave enough to say what they were both thinking.

Many things about Little Leaf Creek still felt foreign to her, but the wonderful friendships she'd made with a handful of people had already made her certain that it was meant to be her home.

Cassie passed a glance toward Sebastian, who sent a curt nod in Oliver's direction. The two had had a few tense moments with Cassie right in the middle of them. Tessa had mentioned that she believed it was because they both liked Cassie, but Cassie couldn't see what either man would see in her. Anyway it wasn't a problem now, Oliver had obviously changed his mind. Cassie turned her attention to him.

"I'm headed over to James' Orchard Store to pick up some produce. Just thought I'd check and see if you needed anything." Oliver swept his gaze over Sebastian once more, then turned his attention back to her.

"Thanks, but I can't think of anything at the

moment." Cassie crouched down to pry open the paint cans.

"James' store?" Sebastian turned to face Oliver. "Why would you go there? Zach's orchard has been in business here for years, and he really needs the support of the community to keep it going, since James has been outselling him."

"James' prices are cheaper." Oliver shrugged as he stared at Sebastian. "I can get a lot more for my money."

"They're cheaper because he's trying to run Zach out of business!" Sebastian's voice roughened as he spoke, though his accent still softened the blow of each word.

"Hey, buy your apples where you want, and I'll buy mine where I want." Oliver rolled his eyes, then pulled the car away from the fence and back onto the road.

Cassie winced as she looked over at Sebastian, but from the stormy expression he wore she guessed he didn't want to talk about it.

That didn't mean she didn't want to hear about it.

"Sit down for a minute, have a muffin." Cassie gestured to the small table and two chairs tucked into the corner of the porch. "I'll get us some iced tea. If we're going to work for a while you should eat first."

"Alright, thank you." Sebastian eased down into one of the wooden chairs and plucked a muffin off of the plate. "Tessa made these?"

"Yes." Cassie glanced back to smile at him, then hurried into the kitchen. She guessed he would be grateful that she wasn't the one who had tried to bake. She hoped that some of Tessa's talent would eventually rub off on her, but so far it hadn't. She returned with two glasses of iced tea and set them down on the table. "Are you alright?" She met his eyes as she sat down across from him.

"Sorry about the attitude." Sebastian pulled his cap off his head and dug his fingers through his thick, blond hair. "It just gets under my skin when people support predators."

"Predators?" Cassie's eyes widened at the thought. "That's what you think of James?"

"I know it sounds harsh. He's new in town, and I do try to keep an open mind about people. But he knows what he's doing when he prices his produce so low, it means that no one else in the area can compete with him. I've seen it happen before, and it's never pretty." Sebastian sighed as he took another bite of the muffin. "It's something I don't have to worry about. I sell most of my produce to one of the big grocery stores, and they're more interested in having a steady source than getting the cheapest price. But some of these orchards and farms, they rely completely on their local sales." He winced. "I saw it coming when Ben died. That orchard has been in his family for a long time, and I knew he intended to pass it down to his children, but they're too interested in the city life to be bothered. So, they turned it over to this outsider." He paused and met her eyes. "No offense."

"None taken." Cassie nodded.

"Anyway, it's all about profit to him. He runs everyone else out of business, he'll buy up their properties once they're in foreclosure, then he'll be the only option." Sebastian shook his head. "No ethics."

Cassie took a sip of tea and glanced away as she felt a pang of guilt. She'd bought her produce from James a few times, because his prices were cheaper. It hadn't occurred to her to think about supporting Zach's business.

"I'm sorry to hear that. I'll be sure to do my best to support Zach from now on."

"I'm sure you will." Sebastian smiled at her, then

stood up. "As much as I enjoy talking with you, we'd better get some work done."

Cassie wondered for a moment if he really did enjoy it, or if that was just his polite way of saying he didn't want to waste his time on chatting. She pushed the insecurity away and reminded herself that it didn't matter either way. Sebastian could be a great friend, and he certainly did know how to fix everything, it was best not to let her mind wander to other things.

CHAPTER 3

Working with Sebastian was easy. He sang along to the music, he offered suggestions to improve her work without it sounding like a criticism, and he didn't mind a little silence now and then. Other than a short break for lunch, they worked the entire day and had the first coat on the front of the house done by the time Sebastian began to pack up his things. He often spent a few hours a day working on the house with her, but he had lots of other commitments running a farm and this was the first full day they had spent together.

"It's looking really good." With her hands on her hips, Cassie took a step back to the edge of the porch to drink in as much of the view of the new color as she could. The rustic red and white reminded her of the houses she had grown up around.

"Team work makes everything better." Sebastian tossed the last of his supplies into the back of his truck. "Tomorrow?"

"Sure thing!" Cassie waved to Sebastian as he pulled away from the house. He'd refused to accept payment, as usual, and she found herself more determined than ever to find a way to make it up to him. Perhaps, a delicious Thanksgiving dinner would offset some of the debt she owed him. The thought of Thanksgiving reminded her of her encounter that morning with Tessa. If only she could get her to even consider attending the dinner, maybe she could break through the shields the woman surrounded herself with long enough to get to know her better. She guessed that Tessa yearned to create a feast, even though she'd refused to participate. She'd seen how calming it was for Tessa to bake. If she could just get her baking, she might soften on the idea of joining in.

"Apple pie." Cassie snapped her fingers and smiled. "That's it. No one can resist a good apple pie. If I can get Tessa to make one of those, it'll put her in the mood for Thanksgiving." She grabbed her keys and slung her purse over her shoulder. A cheerful bounce entered her step as she walked out to her car. To make the best apple pie, she'd have to have some great apples. She hoped it was still early enough for Zach's produce stand to be open.

As Cassie drove out of town along the road that led out to some of the orchards and farms in the area, she felt a sense of nostalgia. She could recall riding in the back of her father's truck, her arms outstretched as she imagined that she could feel the sky against her fingertips. In the city, everywhere she turned, there were buildings as high as she could see. Her only refuge was the penthouse, and their rooftop garden, where she could catch a few peeks of pure sky between the other buildings that surrounded the one she lived in. Over time those patches of sky had become thinner and thinner. Here, the wide open sky greeted her at almost every turn. The sprawling farmland left her enchanted with the idea of endless potential. It was hard not to think of the future, when she was surrounded by so much possibility, and the prickling sensation that she didn't want to be alone any longer.

After her husband, Michael, passed away, she was stunned. She hadn't expected it, and of course she grieved for him. But a part of her opened up, too, a part that she had shut down long ago, the part that even dared to imagine what her life could be like without him. It still inspired a pang of guilt when her mind wandered over those emotions, facing the loss of an important person in her life, in the same moment that she regained a sense of freedom that she had given up on a long time before.

A wooden shop erected in front of James' orchard caught Cassie's attention as she drove past it. A large, colorfully painted sign declared the roadside shop open. It was easy to get to, far more accessible than Zach's, and brand new. After hearing what Sebastian had to say about James, she could see now that this new shop was just another step he'd taken to wipe out Zach's profits. She sighed as she shook her head. At least she could do her best to support Zach, even though her meager purchase wouldn't likely make a difference in the long run.

Cassie drove down the dirt road that led toward Zach's orchard, a little under a mile from James'. As she neared the produce stand, she noticed that the clapboard shutter had already been closed over the front of the shop. A sign on the board declared the stand closed. Her heart sank with disappointment. She wanted to surprise Tessa with the apples the next day. She wouldn't have a chance to get them in the morning.

After a moment of consideration, Cassie turned around in the driveway, and headed back in the direction of James' store. It wouldn't be so terrible to make one purchase, would it? She dismissed the thought. She needed apples, and James had them. She pulled up beside the stand and parked her car. As she stepped out into the mixture of gravel and dirt that surrounded the shop, she didn't see anyone inside.

"Hello?" Cassie noted the sign still announced the shop was open. "Is anyone here?" She opened the door to the shop and peered inside. There were piles of produce in various bins throughout the shop, and a wooden counter with a cash register perched on one end. But no cashier stood behind it.

Frustrated, she stepped back out of the shop. How was it that she'd managed to stop at two shops and still end up with no apples? A quick glance at her watch informed her it was too late to try the grocery store. She wouldn't be back in time. Everything in small towns closed early, that was one part of the slow life that she didn't appreciate. "Hello?" She walked around the side of the shop to the top of the driveway that led down to James' house.

With the sun just beginning to set, the twilight

made it hard to discern shadow from reality, but her eyes focused on a figure in the middle of the driveway. It appeared to be a person, but the person was sprawled out on the ground. Her heart lurched as she realized that the person might be in some kind of trouble. She ran toward the figure, hoping with each step that it would turn out to just be an old sack left behind by a farmhand, or a trick of the faint sunlight that still filtered through the tall trees that lined the driveway.

The closer Cassie got, the more distinct the shape became. Yes, it was a person. A man, to be more specific, who stared up at the sky. His arms were splayed awkwardly out from his sides and one foot was propped up against the packed dirt, as if he had tried to get back up. Bits of light played off of the metal that stuck out from his chest.

Cassie gasped as she reached him. The strange bladed tool was driven so deep that she could only see a few of its serrated teeth above his torn flannel shirt. She grabbed for his wrist, even as her heart sank. No life remained in this man, but she still had to be certain. The skin under her fingertips still held warmth, but no matter how hard she squeezed there was no subtle pounding to be detected.

"Help!" Cassie pushed herself back up to her feet

as she gasped for enough air to make her voice travel farther. "Help! Someone! Please!"

Dazed, Cassie tugged her phone from her purse. Her fingers struggled to type in the code, her heart raced as she managed to punch in the emergency number. As she relayed her location to the calm voice on the other end of the line, three men came running from three different directions, headed straight for her. Her heart lurched as it crossed her mind that any one of them could be the person who took James' life.

Cassie's heart slammed against her chest as the three men drew closer. She didn't recognize any of them, which wasn't a surprise to her, as she hadn't gotten to know too many people, yet. The first man, who appeared to be in his sixties, pulled off his straw hat as he approached her. His eyes remained focused on her.

"Ma'am, are you alright?" He reached for her elbow to steady her, though his own hand trembled as he grasped it.

The second man, perhaps in his thirties stopped short at the sight of James' body on the ground.

"Oh no!" He gasped and looked at the third man. "It's James! He's dead!"

The third man, somewhere in his forties or fifties

eyed the body on the ground and shook his head. He dusted dirt off his hands against his jeans, then crouched down beside James' body.

"What happened here?" He mumbled his words, then lifted his eyes straight up to Cassie. "Did you see what happened?"

"No." Cassie stared back at him as she tried to get her mind to stop spinning. "No, I just wanted to buy some apples." She shoved her phone back into her purse. "The police are on their way."

Sirens echoed through the open land. She planted her feet into the ground in an attempt to remain steady. "Do all of you work here?"

"Yes." The man who still held her elbow spoke in a soothing tone. "I'm Miah, and that's Colin, and Jackson." He nodded to the two other men. Colin, the older man, still stared down at James, his expression frozen between horror and surprise. Jackson, the youngest of the group, passed his palm gently across James' eyes to close them.

"You shouldn't—" Cassie's voice caught in her throat, then she forced the remaining words past. "You shouldn't touch him, the police will need to gather evidence."

"Evidence?" Jackson looked up at her. "Are you saying this was a murder?"

"What else could it be?" Cassie took a step back and pulled her arm away from Miah. As kind as the men were being, she had no idea who they were, or whether they might have been involved in James' death. "That tool didn't end up there by accident."

"It's an edge digger." Colin seemed to wake from his stupor, though his eyes fluttered a few times before he could speak again. "We use them to dig out stubborn roots. They're very sharp."

"He couldn't have fallen on it." Miah shook his head as he surveyed the body. "He's on his back."

"Who would hurt James?" Jackson straightened up and crossed his arms as he stared down at James. "This is crazy. Why wouldn't he have shouted for help?"

"He might have." Miah shook his head and cleared his throat. "We were all out in the orchard, right? We wouldn't have heard him."

"I was down by the creek, working on the fence." Colin narrowed his eyes as he glanced at the other two men. "I didn't hear anything at all, not until I heard your scream." He turned his attention back to Cassie and took a sharp breath. "Did you see who did this to him?"

Cassie took a step back as she felt the weight of all three men's attention settle on her. A thin layer of sweat coated her forehead and cheeks. Her heart launched into an even faster, irregular pattern of beats.

"I didn't see anyone."

"You don't have to be scared." Jackson's steady gaze probed hers. His voice softened. "If you saw someone, we won't let them hurt you. You're safe with us."

Cassie shook her head. "No, I'm not scared. I didn't see anyone."

A wave of dizziness made it impossible for Cassie to focus in on the faces that drew closer to her. Each appeared etched with concern, but the closer they came, the more panicked she felt.

The jarring sound of the slam of a car door broke through the fog of shock that had settled around her senses. She spun on her heel and watched as Oliver strode toward her.

Relief instantly pulsed through her as he came closer. His rigid stance and sharp gaze indicated his only interest was the body on the ground.

A few other police cars pulled in behind his, followed by an ambulance. It crossed her mind that the ambulance was completely unnecessary, but as another wave of dizziness washed away her ability to focus, she wondered if it might be there for her.

"Cassie, I've got you." Oliver's hand grasped her upper arm as she swayed.

Despite him being right next to her, his voice sounded distant.

"James, he's dead." Cassie forced the words past her lips which felt numb and strange.

"She found him like this." Jackson filled in for her, and gripped her other arm for support. "I think she's in shock."

Oliver signaled to the paramedics. "Get a gurney over here!"

"No, I'm okay." Cassie pulled away from their hands, which felt too tight against her skin. "I just need to breathe, I just need some air." She ignored the paramedics as they attempted to evaluate her, and stepped off the side of the road, away from the people and the flashing lights. She leaned her hands against the tops of her knees and sucked down a few deep breaths. Jackson was probably right, she probably was in shock, but she didn't want to be whisked away by any ambulance. She wanted to know what happened to James. This wasn't the first dead body she had seen since moving to Little Leaf Creek, but it was definitely still a shock.

"Cassie, it's best if you get checked out." Oliver's voice held a hint of irritation.

"Please, Oliver." Cassie looked up into his eyes. "I'm okay. Let me stay."

"Only if you sit down." Oliver guided her in the direction of his car. He popped the back driver's side door open and gestured for her to get in. "I need to know that you're okay while I figure out what happened here."

"I'm okay," Cassie muttered the words as she settled in the back seat. She didn't want to be in the back of his police car. She didn't want to be on James' private road, wondering how he had ended up dead. But it was where she was, and there was nothing she could do to change it. She would, however, use the opportunity to find out as much information as she could.

Cassie watched as Oliver made his rounds, questioning the men who had run to her in response to her screams. As she observed their interaction, she wondered why they had heard her, but not James. Hadn't he called out for help? Wouldn't he have screamed just as loud as she did? The thought left her unsettled. Perhaps, the killer didn't give him a chance to scream. James might have felt comfortable with the person who took his life, and was caught by surprise when he was attacked. But that would mean that James knew the person.

Cassie sank back in the seat and closed her eyes.

"You alright there?"

His honey sweet voice seeped through the fear and confusion that wrapped around her. She opened her eyes and looked straight into a familiar deep brown gaze.

"Sebastian? What are you doing here?"

He tilted his head toward the road. "I was passing by, I saw your car up by the stand, and all of the flashing lights. I just wanted to see what was happening. Are you hurt?" He brushed a few brown curls away from her face.

"No, I'm fine." Cassie sighed, as she looked past him to the area that had been roped off with crime scene tape. "But James isn't."

Oliver stepped away from the other officers and back toward his car. He paused beside Sebastian.

"Cassie, are you sure you didn't see anyone else when you arrived?"

"No, I didn't see anyone." Cassie looked down at her hands.

"Not even over by the front of the house? It looks like someone had been digging over there." Oliver crouched down in front of the open car door. "Maybe you wouldn't have noticed when you first walked up."

"I would have noticed." Cassie looked up at him. "I tried to go to Zach's for apples, but he was closed. So, I came back here. The sign said open, but there was no one in the shop, so I walked up the driveway to see if anyone was around." She clasped her hands together. "That's when I saw him."

"I'm sorry you had to see that." Sebastian rested his hand on her shoulder. "Zach doesn't usually close until sunset." He squinted across the wide open space between the two orchards as if he might be able to spot the other man.

"I'll have to find out where he was, maybe he saw something." Oliver signaled to one of the other officers. "I've got enough information from you now. Officer Green will drive you home."

Cassie recoiled at the thought of getting into the car with the officer. She'd seen him a few times, but she barely knew him.

"I'll take her home." Sebastian offered her his hand.

"Is that okay with you, Cassie?" Oliver met her eyes.

"Yes." Cassie took Sebastian's hand and stood up from the car. "Thanks Sebastian."

"No problem." Sebastian gave her a small smile.

"I'll have Officer Green bring your car home for

you." Oliver held his hand out for the keys. "That sound okay?"

"Sure, thanks Oliver." As Cassie handed the keys to him it struck her how lucky she was to have made two good friends in Little Leaf Creek, who had both managed to be there for her when she needed them the most.

CHAPTER 5

Sebastian remained quiet as he started his truck and pulled away from James' orchard. A few minutes into the drive, he glanced over at her.

"Do you need the heat on?" He jabbed a button on the dashboard.

"No, I'm fine," Cassie mumbled, her mind still trying to piece together every single second from her arrival at James' orchard to the moment that she found him on the ground.

Sebastian ran his hand from the curve of her shoulder down to the top of her wrist.

"You're shivering."

His touch left behind strange tingling sensations throughout her arm.

"I'm fine, I'm not cold." Cassie sank down in the seat and squeezed her eyes shut. She knew she was in a state of shock. If only she could calm down, he wouldn't keep looking over at her.

"Scared?" Sebastian whispered the word as he glanced over at her again. Rich brown eyes locked to hers. "It's okay, you're safe now."

Cassie gazed back at him for an instant, then looked out through the windshield.

"I just need some rest. I'm just tired." Cassie wiped her hand across her face and sighed. "I'm sorry, Sebastian."

"Sorry?" Sebastian's eyes narrowed. "What could you possibly be sorry about?"

"I wanted to buy the apples from Zach, but his shop was closed. I really wanted to have them for tomorrow, so I went back to James' shop to buy them. I know I should have bought them from Zach." Cassie's voice sounded strange to her, dreamy and faint, as if she was half-asleep. *Wake up, Cassie, get it together.*

"It doesn't matter, Cassie." Sebastian rubbed his hand along the curve of her shoulder again, then let it settle back against his own knee. "Just close your eyes and relax, I'll have you home shortly."

"I needed the apples to make apple pie." Cassie

leaned her head against the back of the seat and closed her eyes. "Actually, to get Tessa to make apple pie. I thought maybe if she made it, she'd be more likely to want to celebrate Thanksgiving with me."

"Ah, she hasn't done that since she moved back to Little Leaf Creek." Sebastian shook his head as he turned down the street that led to Cassie's house. "Tessa moved away after her friend died, and since she's returned she pretty much keeps to herself really, at least, until you moved in."

Finally, more of the mystery around Tessa was starting to be revealed. The reason she had left Little Leaf Creek was because her friend had died. Cassie already knew that she had left Little Leaf Creek and worked in a police department a few towns over. Oliver had gone to the same area to the police academy and worked in a few different police departments, including the one where Tessa had worked. But she never knew why Tessa had left Little Leaf Creek in the first place.

"Alice, right?" Cassie's eyes fluttered open as she glanced over at him.

"Yes." Sebastian eased the car to a stop in her driveway. "Let's get you inside." He unbuckled his seat belt, then walked around to the passenger side of the truck. As he helped her down, his hand landed on the slope of her waist to steady her.

"I'm okay, really." Cassie pulled away from his touch, shocked by the bolt of electricity it sent through her. "Can you come in for a minute? For some iced tea?"

"Sure." Sebastian nodded as he glanced up at the house. "I want to make sure you're all settled."

"You must think I can't handle much of anything. Can't handle fixing up my own house, can't handle buying some apples." Cassie shook her head as she mounted the stairs.

"I don't think that at all, Cassie." Sebastian followed right behind her. "I think you've had quite a shock and might need some company until your nerves settle a little. Honestly, I didn't even see what you saw, and my nerves are rattled just thinking of poor James. I wish I hadn't been so harsh to him now."

Cassie glanced back over her shoulder as she unlocked the door and noticed a wince flicker across his features. He really did feel guilty.

"Maybe you didn't like the way James conducted business, but that doesn't mean you wished him any harm." Cassie pushed the door open and stepped inside. The silence made the house feel empty.

Sebastian stepped in behind her, and she felt as if his presence, warm and determined, filled up all the space around her. He was right, she did need his company.

"I'll get us some iced tea." Cassie walked toward the kitchen.

"Cassie, please sit down." Sebastian gestured to the couch not far from the front door. "I can get the tea."

"I can do it." Cassie sighed as she noted the frustration that creased his brow. "We can do it together. I need to move around a bit and get my blood flowing. If I just sit and stare, I'll never get it together."

"Fair enough." Sebastian followed her into the kitchen and accepted the glasses she handed him.

"I'm glad you came by when you did. I wasn't looking forward to riding home with a strange police officer." Cassie shook her head. "I'm sure that he's a good man, but it's nice to have a friend close by at a time like this."

"I feel the same way." Sebastian set the glasses on the table as she carried the pitcher of tea to it.

"Did you know James well?" Cassie noticed a tremble in her hand as she poured the tea. She tightened her muscles and managed not to splash any of the sweet liquid out of the glass.

"Not really. He hadn't been here long, and I was on Zach's side of things. I did approach him once, just to talk things over. I thought he might listen to reason, maybe he just didn't understand how things work around here." Sebastian sat down in one of the chairs at the table.

"Of course you did." Cassie smiled as she set the pitcher back in the fridge. "You are always trying to make things better."

"If I can." Sebastian met her eyes as she sat down across from him. "Is that a bad thing?"

"Not at all." Cassie looked back at him. "I think it's a wonderful trait."

"Good." Sebastian smiled.

"I'm working on a project."

"A project?"

"I'm trying to distract myself right now, so hear me out."

"Alright." Sebastian sat back in his chair, a smile tugged at the corners of his lips.

"I don't think that Tessa should be alone for Thanksgiving, so I'm trying to get her to come over." Cassie took a sip of her tea, then set the glass back down.

"The apple pie." Sebastian smiled some. "It seems like I'm not the only one that likes to make things better around here."

"I just want to try and get her to be more relaxed and open." Cassie smiled.

"Good luck with that. Tessa has always been standoffish. But if she invites you in, she treats you like family." Sebastian stood up from his chair. "You might not want to push it though, or you might find yourself on the outside."

CHAPTER 6

Sebastian's warning echoed through Cassie's thoughts as she tried to sleep that night, between memories of her own screams for help when she came across James' body. With so much to keep her tossing and turning she'd barely had any sleep when the alarm went off.

There was no reason to begin chipping wallpaper off of the wall in the living room as soon as she woke. Yet, that's exactly what she did. There were so many projects in the house to work on, and she didn't have much time before work, but she felt compelled to get out the scraper and go at it.

As Cassie peeled away the faded paper, she felt her muscles tense and vibrate with the movement. The quicker she moved her hands, the more relaxed her mind became, and the images from the night before slowed from a swirl to a steady parade. What happened to James? Who had killed him? How could she find out the truth?

A knock on the front door made her jump. The scraper fell from her hand as she spun around to face the figure on the other side of the screen. She'd opened the wooden front door to let the air circulate through the screen door, though it hadn't done much to keep her cool.

"Ollie."

He pushed the door open some.

"Sorry, did I scare you?"

"Just surprised me." Cassie waved her hand as she walked toward the door. "I wasn't expecting anyone."

"I wanted to check in on you." Oliver stood in the doorway, his eyes surveying the living room. Although, she had brought some furniture with her when she had moved to Little Leaf Creek, she still hadn't completely furnished the house. She wanted to get the place fixed-up before she did. The walls were bare, and the furniture was sparse.

"Thanks for that." Cassie pushed her hair back from her sweaty forehead and met his eyes. "I'm doing okay."

"Are you sure?" Oliver took a step through the door. "What you saw last night, it's a lot to take in."

"I know it is." Cassie frowned as the memory flashed through her mind. "But I'm more concerned about finding out the truth about what happened to James."

"I'm working on that." Oliver lifted a bag that he had been holding behind his back. "I know you said you went to the stand to buy apples." He held the bag out to her. "I picked these up from James yesterday. I thought you might like to have them."

"Thank you." Cassie smiled as she took the bag. "That's so thoughtful. But don't you need them? How much do I owe you for them?"

"I've got some at home. I just bought some more because he had a good price on them. This time of year always makes me crave apples. You don't owe me anything." Oliver's lips tightened into a thin line, then he sighed. "I keep going over the time I spent there and wondering if I missed something. Was there some sign that he was in trouble?"

"If there was, I'm sure that you would have noticed it." Cassie set the bag of apples on the table. "It's crossed my mind that if I had stopped at James' shop first, I might have been able to help him. Instead, I went to Zach's. It's hard not to think of the ways this could have been prevented, but the truth is only one person could have stopped it, and that is the killer. That's where the blame lies."

"You're right about that." Oliver coasted his hand across the slope of his cheek. "I'm glad you didn't stop there first. You could have been in danger. You need to be careful now, everyone is a suspect."

"So, Zach is a suspect? I thought it was odd that Zach's stand was closed." Cassie said, as she considered whether Zach could be the murderer. Would he take a chance like that? Wouldn't he know that he'd be suspected? Maybe he never thought it through. He might have confronted James, and things may have gotten out of hand.

"Yes, it should have been open. We're investigating all avenues at the moment." Oliver ruffled his hand through his hair.

Cassie realized that Oliver did think Zach was a suspect even though he didn't come right out and say it.

"But if it was Zach, surely he would know he would be suspected."

"People don't always make the smartest decisions when they are angry."

"True." Cassie bit into her bottom lip, then shook her head. "What about the murder weapon? If it was someone that didn't work on the property, they would have had to bring that with them, which means they planned to at least hurt James, right?" She noticed the conflict in Oliver's expression.

"Actually, we think the tool was there. We found an area near the porch where someone had been digging. My guess is it was James. The killer came up to him, confronted him, got the tool away from him, and used it to kill him." Oliver licked his lips as he glanced down at the floor, then back up at her. "It might have even been self-defense. Maybe James attacked his killer first, and the killer fought back. Everything is still being investigated right now. It's going to take some time to sort through it all. But I'd say the one thing I'm pretty certain of, is that it was someone James knew. Someone who knew him, and knew his property. Of course that doesn't narrow down the suspect list too much."

"No, but it's a start." Cassie's mind filled with visions of the scenario that Oliver described. Was it James who was the aggressor? He was known to have a bit of a temper.

"You say you only saw the three farmhands there, right? No other cars pulling away? No strange sounds in the distance?"

"Just them." Cassie nodded. "And they didn't

come until I called for help. Whoever killed James most probably took off on foot, because I didn't hear any car engines, motorcycles, nothing. I have a tendency to notice little things, and I didn't notice any of that."

"We fanned out and tried to set up a perimeter but the orchards are so large it's hard to contain them." Oliver sighed. "Alright, well I'd better get back to it. Are you going to take it easy today?"

"Actually, I have to work this morning, then I'm going to spend some time with Tessa." Cassie caught herself before she could share her plan to coax Tessa into sharing Thanksgiving with her. She guessed that Oliver might be just as hard to convince. "Do you have any holiday plans?"

"Holiday?" Oliver blinked, then gave a short laugh. "Oh Thanksgiving, no. I'll probably be working."

"I'm hoping to have a small get together. I'd love for you to come, if you'd be willing. You could stop by anytime if you're working." Cassie tried to meet his eyes as he looked away.

"Uh, thanks. Maybe. We'll see." Oliver shrugged, then turned toward the door. "Until all of this is settled, please be extra careful, Cassie. It's possible that whoever killed James saw you, and might suspect that you know more than you're saying. Just be cautious."

"I hadn't thought of that." Cassie frowned. "I will be."

Oliver waved over his shoulder as he turned to leave.

Cassie bent down to pick up the scraper she'd dropped, as her hand reached for it, her mind flashed back to the tool that had been wedged into James' chest.

Determined not to lose her focus, Cassie decided a shower would be good before work. As she washed away the sweat from tearing at the wallpaper, her thoughts returned to the three men that had approached her when she called for help. They were all in different parts of the orchard, which meant that maybe one of them had witnessed something. It was a place to start. If she could stay focused on finding the killer, she might be able to leave the shock of finding James the way she did, behind her. Then maybe she really could recreate the kind of Thanksgiving that she could recall from her small town childhood.

CHAPTER 7

For many years before Cassie moved to Little Leaf Creek, her main job had been to manage her husband's social schedule, as well as her own. It hadn't exactly been easy, but she did find it very boring. Working as the manager of a small museum was more exciting, but that wasn't her main focus. She enjoyed the job but never got close to anybody.

Now that she was back to working as a waitress, as she once had in her hometown, she found the idea of going into work to be exciting. However, knowing that she would likely be the main topic of discussion, filled her with dread instead. She pushed open the door to the diner and a hush fell over the once chattering crowd. Her cheeks flushed as she lowered her head and pretended not to know the sudden silence was about her. Of course, word had gotten around that she had stumbled across James' body, that meant she was just as much a part of the gossip. Once she walked over to the front counter, the conversations picked back up.

"Hey there, sweetheart." Mirabel Light leaned against the counter as she smiled at her. "Rough day yesterday?"

"You could say that." Cassie pulled her apron off of the hook near the kitchen door and sighed as she draped it over her head. "I guess everyone knows?"

"Trust me, it's better than having to retell the story over and over to every curious person." Mirabel lowered her voice as she leaned in close to her. "Don't let anyone bait you into it, they've all heard it a thousand times by now."

"Thanks for the advice." Cassie tied the apron tight around her waist and shook her head. "I just wish it never happened."

"Of course you do." Mirabel patted Cassie's shoulder, then brushed a few strands of her hair back from her face. "Just remember, there was nothing that you could have done. James had his enemies, and I'm sure his choices led him to his final moments."

"You're saying you think it was his fault?" Cassie's eyes widened as she stared into Mirabel's.

"Not exactly." Mirabel frowned. "No one asks to be murdered, but he knew how to stir up trouble. A few weeks ago, he was in here with Ben's kids, and they were getting into it. James was being downright nasty if you ask me. Those kids lost their father, and they didn't need James yelling in their faces."

"Ben, he's the one who owned the orchard before James, right?" Cassie crossed her arms as she leaned against the counter beside her. "What does James have to do with them?"

"They struck some kind of deal. James bought the orchard from them, but they are still partial owners somehow. I don't know, I don't know the details of it all. All I know is that Ben wanted that orchard to stay in his family, and maybe those kids should have tried harder to honor his wishes." Mirabel waved to a customer who walked in. "We're pretty busy, Cassie, better get to those tables before they decide not to leave you any tips."

"Right, I'm going right now." Cassie gazed at Mirabel for a moment longer, then turned her attention to the waiting diners. After taking a flurry of orders and delivering several drinks, she finally had a second to catch her breath. Only a second, before a large group in their early twenties made their way through the door. Cassie recognized a few of them as friends of Trevor Danel's, the young artist that had created the statue in her front yard. Once she had them settled at a table, she prepared to take their order.

"What can I get for you?" As Cassie looked up from the notebook she held, she noticed that all five of them stared straight at her. Her heart skipped a beat as she realized they were there for more than food. Still, she jotted down each item that they ordered and did her best to remain friendly, despite their stares. "I'll be right back with your order." She turned toward the kitchen, but before she could take a step, one of the young men called out to her.

"Cassie. You're the Cassie, right? The one that found the body?"

Her shoulders tensed as she turned back to face him.

"I was there yesterday, yes."

One of the girls, her hair long and bright blue, met her eyes. "I knew it was you."

"I'd better get your order in." Cassie hurried away from the group and did her best to avoid them until their order was ready.

As Cassie delivered their food to the table, she sensed their interest again.

"So, what was it like?" The girl with the blue hair scooted her chair closer to the edge of the table and looked into Cassie's eyes. "When you found him?"

"It was terrible." Cassie took a slight step back, then shook her head. "I just can't imagine anyone murdering someone."

"Oh, I can." An older boy kicked his feet up on the chair next to him and grinned. "I know plenty of people that wanted to get rid of him. All of the workers from that orchard that he fired the moment he took it over. He only kept on the workers that had been there the longest because he knew they had the most experience to keep the business going and train him in it. And he could force them out by next season. He knew he could work them harder and save money. People were counting on those jobs, and they lost a lot when James fired them." He raised his eyebrows. "My dad for one."

"I'm sorry to hear that he had so much trouble." Cassie chose her words carefully as she studied him. "Was he able to find something new?"

"Nope, and we had to move out of our house and into my grandparents' place." He pursed his lips. "It's a tight fit."

"Keep quiet, Duncan, you're going to make your dad a suspect." The boy beside him elbowed him.

"He already is." Duncan shrugged. "Police were by my place this morning. But you didn't see him out there did you, Cassie?"

"I only saw three workers there. What's your dad's name?" Cassie asked, trying to keep her voice even.

"Nathan." Duncan leaned closer to her.

"No, I didn't see him." Cassie's heart skipped a beat as Duncan's eyes bored into hers.

"Good. Because he wasn't there." Duncan picked up a fry from his plate and chomped down on it.

"I'm sure the police will have it sorted out in no time." Cassie took a breath and reminded herself that they were barely more than children. Of course they were intrigued, and a little excited. It was normal for their age. "We all just have to think about the family that he left behind."

"Why?" Duncan leaned back in his chair as he looked at her. "He didn't think of our families when he fired everyone with no notice, did he?"

Cassie opened her mouth to speak, but Mirabel summoned her before she could.

"I need some help over here, Cassie, if you're not

busy." Mirabel pointed to some half-empty bottles of ketchup.

"Excuse me." Cassie forced a smile at the group, then turned and walked over to the counter. She knew the call for help had been a rescue mission, the ketchup bottles were just fine, and would be filled at the end of the shift. "Thanks Mirabel."

"I thought you might have had enough of their questions." Mirabel frowned as she looked over at the group. "They're mostly harmless, but Duncan, he likes to cause trouble and vandalize things. Hopefully, he grows out of it soon."

"He seems pretty angry about what happened to his dad. Do you know him?" Cassie gathered the bottles and carried them behind the counter.

"Nathan, sure. He lost a lot when James fired him, all of the workers did. Ben took such good care of them, he paid them what he could, but he showed them respect. He would never have let them go with no notice. A lot of the men that worked for him had records that stopped them from getting other jobs, but Ben never treated them bad for it." Mirabel frowned as she poured out some old coffee and prepared to brew a fresh pot. "Oliver is going to have his hands full narrowing down the suspects on this one."

"I'm sure he will." Thinking of Oliver sparked a thought about Tessa. "I'm hoping to get Tessa to have Thanksgiving with me. In fact, I'd love for you to come, too." She smiled at the thought. "Wouldn't it be nice to have dinner served to you for once?"

"Tempting." Mirabel narrowed her eyes. "If you can convince her, I'll be there."

"Great. Now there is even more of a reason to make sure she comes." Cassie smiled.

Mirabel straightened up. "Alright, back to work for both of us. There's a lot to get ready for the lunch rush."

Cassie began to prep things for lunch, but her thoughts wandered back to the murder.

CHAPTER 8

At the end of her shift, Cassie decided to go to Tessa's. She stopped at her house long enough to grab the bag of apples that Oliver gave her, then walked over to Tessa's house. The goats barely lifted their heads in her direction as she climbed the steps. After a light knock on the door, Tessa opened it, and greeted her with a warm smile. "I was hoping to see you."

"Here I am." Cassie grinned as she stepped inside. "I brought these." She held up the bag of apples and looked into Tessa's eyes.

"Oh, that's sweet, but I think I would have much preferred wine or chocolate." Tessa winked as she took the bag from Cassie.

"I brought them because I am hoping that you'll

teach me how to make apple pie." Cassie sweetened her voice as much as possible as she followed Tessa into the kitchen.

"So, this is a bribe?" Tessa set the bag down and turned to face Cassie. "Or a trap?"

"I want to make a meal for Thanksgiving now that I'm in my new home." Cassie held up her hands as Tessa opened her mouth. "I know, I know, you don't want to come. But I had hoped you might still be willing to share your recipe with me. You know I will just burn whatever I try to bake!"

"I'm sure you would do just fine." Tessa pursed her lips. "I know a trap when I see one."

"Listen, I want to make a good impression on my first Thanksgiving. Just help me out, please?" Cassie plopped down in one of the chairs at the kitchen table and rubbed behind Harry's ears. "We can talk while we bake. I need to figure out what happened to James so I can concentrate on the holiday."

"Holidays are just an invention of the capitalist system." Tessa huffed, then grabbed some supplies from the cabinets. "One of these days you'll realize that."

"I hope not." Cassie frowned as she pulled out her notebook. "I think it's great when friends and family get together and share what's going on with their lives over a wonderful meal."

"Maybe." Tessa's voice had a wistful tone. She handed her a bowl. "Peel the apples, careful not to take off too much of the apple meat itself."

"Okay, I can do that." Cassie got to work on the apples as she shared with her what she'd found out at work. "So, it does sound like there was an issue between James and Ben's kids. But something about the way Duncan behaved made me uneasy. I can't help but wonder if his dad knows something or maybe was even involved."

"He'd certainly have good reason to want some revenge. But it seems like an odd place and time to take it. Maybe he confronted James and things got out of hand?" Tessa shook her head. "It's hard to say, but he should definitely go on the list. If it were me, I'd start with those that you know were there."

"Time to start a list." Cassie set down the apple in her hand and picked up her pen. She wrote out the names of the people she suspected so far, from Ben's kids, to the fired employees, to the three men who were working on the property at the time of James' death. "Miah, one of the workers, was down working on a fence near the creek." She added that note beneath his name.

"Oh, that fence." Tessa winced as she used her fingers to crumble the flour and butter together for the pie crust. "It's been a thorn in the side of James' neighbors ever since he moved in there. Ben always respected the fact that everyone should have easy access to the creek. But James insisted that the creek was on his property, so he shouldn't have to let them onto it to use it. His neighbors were pretty upset by the idea of him putting a fence around it. They could still access it, but it meant having to go to the other end of their properties, which made things so much harder for them."

"Upset enough to kill?" Cassie jotted down the information about the neighbors.

"I'd like to say no." Tessa pulled the dough together into a ball and turned to look at Cassie. "I'd like to say that nothing is worth taking another life, but the truth is, the answer is yes. When it comes to property fights around here, people can get pretty vicious."

"You know, for keeping to yourself so much, you certainly do seem to keep track of what is going on around here." Cassie looked up from her notebook and raised an eyebrow.

"Once a cop, always a cop." Tessa winked, then formed the dough into a ball. "I might have a police scanner as well." She formed the dough into two disks and wrapped them in plastic wrap, then placed them in the fridge.

"That makes sense." Cassie smiled, then tapped her pen on the notebook. "Any particular neighbor that you think might be eager to get some revenge, or stop the building of the fence?"

"My instincts tell me that Kent Kettler might be someone to look into. His family has owned the farm for generations and his entire focus is on his farm. I think anything that might have threatened his success would get him pretty worked up. Without easy access to the creek for his livestock to drink from, and to water his fields, his business would have suffered, or he would have had to invest in an alternative water source which would have been expensive." Tessa grabbed the peeled apples. "It doesn't amount to a reason to murder someone, to me, but I've seen people murder for much less."

"You never talk about your time on the police force." Cassie watched as Tessa sliced the apples.

"I'm not wearing a badge anymore." Tessa gestured for her to come closer. "If you really want to learn how to make this pie, this is the important part."

"I'm listening." Cassie stood up and walked over to her.

"I'm a big believer in cooking the apples a bit first. Most people will tell you that is the worst thing you can do, but it ensures that they're cooked, and I don't like undercooked apples or soggy pies. Now, we need to make sure it's sweet. To do that we need a good helping of brown sugar." Tessa pointed out a bowl of brown sugar. "Go on, toss it in."

"All of it?" Cassie raised her eyebrows.

"Who asked who for apple pie advice?"

"Okay, okay." Cassie poured the sugar into the apples.

"Now mix it. And add the spices while you're at it."

Cassie followed Tessa's instructions. Stirring the apples was almost as satisfying as the scent that wafted up from the bowl.

"Now, I cook this in the butter for a few minutes." Tessa added the mixture to the melted butter in the pan.

Cassie crinkled up her nose as she looked up in the direction of the strong scent that cut through the sweet.

"What is that?" She eyed the spoonful of liquid in Tessa's hand. She guessed that it was some kind of acid, but it didn't smell like lemon juice. She'd never heard of anyone putting something like that in apple pie and wondered what it would do to the flavor.

"It's a secret." Tessa looked up at her, then added the liquid to the pan. "This is a very special recipe to me, taught to me by someone I held very dear."

Cassie bit into her bottom lip to stop herself from asking if it was Alice. She didn't want to upset Tessa.

"Will you tell me the secret ingredient?"

"I'll give you some time to try figure it out yourself, first." Tessa winked at her. "You can stir."

Cassie stirred the mixture as Tessa began tidying up. She walked over to Cassie and tested one of the apples.

"That looks about ready. We don't want to overcook it." Tessa pointed to a glass bowl. "Pour it in there. When it's cool I'll put it in the fridge overnight." She brushed a wave of her silver hair away from her eyes and smiled. "Tomorrow, we'll bake the pie."

"Thanks for your help, Tessa." Cassie started to turn toward the door.

"You're welcome. But don't think this means I'm coming to Thanksgiving. It doesn't." Tessa narrowed her eyes slightly.

Cassie patted Harry on his head, then stepped out through the back door and crossed the yard into her own. As she glanced back over her shoulder at Tessa's house, she felt an urgency to earn her trust. When she'd begun her mission to convince Tessa to come to Thanksgiving, she'd thought she was doing it for her, and for Oliver. But she was beginning to realize that she needed to have connections in the community. She needed people she could trust. She needed the roots that having people care about you, who you cared about, provided.

CHAPTER 9

Cassie placed her microwaved meal on the side table next to the couch and gave it a few minutes to cool as she set up her computer. Her discussion with Tessa still played through her mind. She needed to find a way to narrow down the suspects, or at least to get an idea of who the best ones were.

"If Zach is a suspect, then that is where I should start." She consulted her list briefly, although she had memorized the reasons why she suspected him. She needed more than what was scrawled across the paper. Yes, he had motive, but that didn't mean that he'd done it, it just meant that he had a reason to do it. She turned her attention to her computer and began to search the local social media pages for any posts that Zach had made. She found several advertising his apples, along with other produce he grew on his land. As she dug a little deeper, she came across a few posts on a local public forum for the town. These were not about his produce, but instead, about James' prices.

Although Zach's posts were fairly professional in language, he made sure his point got across. He insisted that James had been engaging in predatory pricing, with the intent of bankrupting the other orchards in and around Little Leaf Creek. He said that it wasn't just his funds that were taking a hit, but other farmers in the area as well. James continued to undercut the prices of everyone in the area, so that people would only purchase their produce from him. A few people in the community countered his posts with comments about lowering his prices, if he wanted to keep his customers.

Zach responded with a lengthy post about how his finances worked, and the amount of money it took to run his orchard. He pointed out again that the only reason James could offer those prices was because he was selling his produce for less than it cost him to grow it. He was using his own funds to make up the difference, for the sole purpose of eliminating his competition.

This sparked a debate as to whether this was a legal or ethical way to do business.

As Cassie scrolled through the debate she came across a few posts from Sebastian, who supported Zach's point of view. He suggested that the town's entire culture was under threat, because people were choosing to save a few pennies, over supporting their community.

Cassie sat back and closed her eyes for a moment. She could hear Sebastian's voice as she recalled his words from the post. Yes, his docile tone would be tinged with anger as he spoke about the businesses that had closed due to lack of support. Sebastian had a passionate streak when it came to protecting others. For a moment her admiration for him distracted her from the matter at hand. The flash of his wide smile, the determination in his dark brown stare, his eagerness to help, however he could. She shook her head and sighed.

"Focus Cassie, you're wasting time." After a deep breath, and an attempt to clear her mind, a new idea surfaced.

Following her hunch, Cassie decided to look up James' name on the local forum to see if he had ever defended himself against Zach's accusations. Although she didn't find any posts from James himself, she did find more posts that mentioned him, and the property he owned.

The topic of the posts focused on a complaint filed with the historical society regarding the renovations occurring on the property. James had apparently decided to make some changes to the home, and a few people had gathered together in an attempt to garner support for a petition to force him to stop.

As Cassie skimmed over the names that showed support for the petition, her heart skipped a beat. Colin? The same Colin that worked for James? Why would he show his support against the renovations? Maybe it was another Colin?

Cassie jotted a note down on her list, beside Colin's name. As she yawned she decided she would find out more from the historical society first thing in the morning.

At the moment what she needed was sleep, as her muddled thoughts had stopped swimming in different directions, and were now just a pool of nonsense.

Cassie closed the computer, then carried out her bedtime routine. Maybe if she could get some sleep her mind would be clearer in the morning.

As Cassie stretched out in her bed and looked up

at the ceiling, her thoughts drifted back to Tessa, and the pie crust and filling she'd created. She'd insisted that Cassie wouldn't get her way. But Cassie still hoped she might. She thought back to what her previous Thanksgivings had been like. During her years married to Michael, Thanksgiving had felt stiff, uniform, and disappointing. She'd order the same food, from the same caterers, and invite whoever would be best for his business. She'd pour the same wine, endure the same jokes, and do her best not to fall asleep in her mashed potatoes.

Before that, before she'd left home to explore life in the big city, Thanksgiving had been entirely different. It had been loud, and chaotic. Something always ended up burning, but still tasted delicious. There were children everywhere, and grandparents eager to pinch cheeks and tell stories. Beer flowed along with wine, and fruit punch. People laughed, so hard that they risked falling out of their chairs. People argued, so loud, that they got kicked out of the kitchen and into the yard. It wasn't perfect, but it was real, and she longed for those experiences again. She longed for a sense that she belonged somewhere, that she could be surrounded by the young, and the old, by laughter, and by tears, and somehow fit into the middle of all of it.

CHAPTER 10

After a quick breakfast the following morning, Cassie headed for the office of the local historical society. She guessed that if anyone would have more information about the complaints filed, it would be them, and from past encounters with them she knew that they were usually pretty eager to talk about their work to keep the town's integrity intact.

As Cassie stepped into the office, she braced herself for who might be seated behind the desk. She got along with some of the members of the society, but others she had a harder time connecting with. A surge of relief rushed through her at the sight of Avery, one of the youngest members of the society.

"Good morning, Avery." Cassie smiled as she held

out the cup of coffee she'd picked up on her way over. "I thought you might enjoy this."

"Thanks so much!" Avery smiled as she took the cup of coffee. "That's so thoughtful of you." She quirked an eyebrow as she looked up from the coffee. "And I'm guessing it's not free?"

"Avery, of course it is." Cassie offered an innocent shrug. "Why wouldn't it be?"

"I know you were the one who discovered James' body. I also know that you like to dig into things." Avery sat down behind her desk. "So, let's skip the small talk, and get right into it. What are you looking for?"

"Okay." Cassie pulled up a chair to Avery's desk and sat down in it. "I'd like to know about any complaints filed against James regarding the renovations of his property."

"Is that all?" Avery smirked, then shook her head. "Easy enough to find. Just give me a minute." Her fingers flew across the keyboard. "Here we go. Actually, there was only one complaint officially filed." She looked over at her as she picked up her cup of coffee. "One of his employees, Colin Millers, organized the petition and filed the complaint."

So, Cassie had been right, it was one of the three men on the farm that ran to her when she found

James' body, that had not only supported but instigated the petition.

"It strikes me as odd that an employee would organize the petition." Cassie shook her head. "Can you tell me more about the complaint that was filed?"

"I can do you one better." Avery smiled as she stood up and walked over to a tall filing cabinet in the corner of the room. "I can get you a copy of it." She pulled open one of the long drawers. "What's your interest in it?" She lifted an eyebrow as she glanced back at Cassie. "Do you think it had something to do with the murder?"

"I'm just curious." Cassie lowered her eyes, hoping to hide the truth. Although she'd gotten to know the people of Little Leaf Creek, she was still a stranger in their eyes, an outsider, and she didn't want to cause that divide to get any bigger.

"Me too!" Avery snatched a file out of the drawer, then whacked it with her hip. The drawer slammed shut as she held the file out to Cassie. "Everyone is, I think. What could have happened to James? It's not like he was a small man. He would have put up a pretty good fight. Did it look like he had put up a fight?"

Bewildered by the woman's excitement, Cassie

took a breath to hide her shock. Not unlike the teens that had been so eager to hear about the murder, Avery's eyes glistened with interest. For the first time she wondered if she looked the same way when she asked for information about the complaint against James.

"Not to me, it didn't. But I'm sure Detective Graham will figure out whether there was any kind of struggle."

"Sure, Ollie is a great detective. But I watch enough crime shows to have my own suspicions. James was an outsider you know, that puts him at risk in a town like this." Avery's cheeks flushed as her eyes widened. "Not that you should be concerned, of course."

"Thanks." Cassie tightened her grip on the file and did her best to ignore the implications of Avery's words. "I'm sure I'll be just fine. But it is important to find out the truth about what happened to James."

"Oh, yes it is, you wouldn't believe the rumors flying around this town right now. I think every kind of story that you could invent has been invented at this point about what happened to James. If we don't find out the truth, I'm sure it'll become one of those small town legends that people will be talking about for decades." Avery sat back down in her chair and sighed. "I only wish people were as interested in preserving the history of this town as they are in gossiping over current events."

"That's why I'm here. I know how observant all of you are, and how important the town is to you." Cassie met Avery's eyes. "I wanted to know more about the complaint, but I also want to know what you think. Did you notice anything out of the ordinary about James' property? Anything that might have made him a target?"

"I found this section of the complaint particularly interesting. It's about getting rid of the front porch." Avery took a sip of her coffee, then continued. "You see, I remember when Ben first filed for a permit for this porch about eight years ago. I was a new member of the historical society, so I was doing most of the grunt work at the time." She gave a short laugh. "I guess not much has changed in eight years. He was quite determined that the porch would meet all of the regulations and standards for approval. He was so eager to get the project done, he even agreed to spend extra money on high quality wood that the council had requested. We expected a fight, as he was notorious for wanting to save a penny, but instead he agreed to the request immediately. Colin had worked on Ben's orchard from day one and I guess he felt a loyalty to Ben and wanted to ensure that the porch wasn't destroyed and the historical guidelines were followed for the property."

"It is quite beautiful." Cassie looked at a picture of the porch right after it had been completed.

"With Ben gone now, maybe Colin has a sentimental attachment to the house and the porch."

"That would make sense." Cassie pulled out her notebook and jotted down another note under Colin's name. Was his attachment to Ben and the house enough motive to want to kill James? "What doesn't make sense to me is that if the porch was only built eight years ago, and if he did such a good job with it, I mean it still looks absolutely gorgeous, why would James want to change it?" She looked up from the picture in time to see a flicker of annoyance pinch the skin between Avery's eyebrows.

"He wanted to expand the house. He had to remove the front porch to do that. Of course, that's very difficult to do and stay within the regulations."

"So, it was denied?" Cassie set the picture back down in the file and shook her head. "Then why was Colin still upset about it?"

"It wasn't exactly denied." Avery sighed, then

framed her face with her hands. "If it were up to me it would have been denied, but of course it's not just up to me. It's up to the entire society."

"Who could have a different opinion, though?" Cassie narrowed her eyes. "It goes against the regulations."

"It does, but he modified his plans enough that some of the members voted it through. He donated a lot to the historical society so I think that helped." Avery looked into Cassie's eyes. "It's not something I can say I'm proud to be a part of, but it's not as if there are a lot of funds in this small town, and I guess the majority of the society felt that the benefit outweighed the harm."

"So, he paid the council to get what he wanted?" Cassie swallowed hard in an attempt to hide the contempt in her voice. Clearly, it wasn't Avery's fault.

"He supported the council." Avery glanced toward the door of the office, then lowered her voice. "We were still going to insist on certain standards, we basically approved the destruction of the porch, since that wasn't part of the original home, and then he planned to expand the house outward. He was going to harvest the front of the house and do his best to reuse it to keep as much of the authenticity in the home as he could. He was actually making quite an effort. But he wanted the house to be bigger." She shrugged. "Some people aren't satisfied unless they are living in a mansion."

Cassie cringed as she recalled the luxuries of her own penthouse apartment in the city. When she'd first seen it, she'd burst out laughing at the thought of living in it, until she realized her husband was quite serious about purchasing it. Yes, she knew what wealth could do to expectations. She thanked Avery for her time, and the information, then decided to see if she could find out anything from James' neighbors.

As Cassie navigated the thin, dirt roads that connected the properties around James' orchard, she imagined him among the gnarled branches, checking on his harvest, or with his hands deep in the soil, evaluating its nutrients. Had he really loved the land? Had he loved it the way that Ben and his father before him had? Or was the idea of owning an orchard just another check on his list of things to do? She shook off the thought as she headed in the direction of the neighbor that Tessa had mentioned. As she pulled into his driveway, she was surprised to see Tessa's jeep parked out front. She noticed Tessa on the front porch, just as she raised her hand to knock on the door.

"Tessa?" Cassie stepped out of the car, her eyes wide.

"Cassie, what are you doing here?" Tessa stepped back from the door. Although she hadn't knocked, the door swung open.

"Tessa?" The man gazed out at her, his brows knitted with confusion. "What are you doing here?"

"Sorry to bother you, Kent. I just thought I'd drop by and see how you are." Tessa turned to face him.

"You thought you'd stop by to see how I am?" Kent squinted at her. "Are you feeling alright?" He looked past her to Cassie. "Does she need an ambulance?" Cassie recognized him from the diner.

"Alright, alright, enough." Tessa shook her head, then stepped closer to him. "I may prefer to be alone, but that doesn't mean I don't have the right to check on friends when something terrible happens to their neighbor. We're friends aren't we, Kent?" She tilted her head to the side and peered into his eyes.

"Uh, sure, I guess." Kent trailed his fingertips along the curve of his jaw, his lips pursed as he studied her. "It's nice of you to come out and check on me."

"Thanks, now you can invite me inside." Tessa started to step past him.

"Just a second." Kent pulled the door closed

behind him. "Look, I don't know what you two are up to, but just like I told the police, unless you have a search warrant, you aren't coming into my house."

"Now, who's the loner?" Tessa chuckled, then glanced at Cassie. "Not very courteous is he?"

"Kent, we just want to know about your dispute with James Rallow. About the fence he was building." Cassie stepped onto the porch beside Tessa. "It'll be a lot quicker if you just tell us about it." She felt a faint thrill at the thought of standing beside Tessa while she questioned Kent. It wasn't the first time they had spoken to a suspect together, but she always got the same feeling of excitement. Tessa's experience as a police officer, actually carrying out investigations, made Cassie feel more confident that they could find out the truth.

"Is that so?" Kent turned his attention on Cassie. "I've heard you two have been spending too much time together. You have to watch out for this one, Cassie. Sometimes she forgets that she surrendered her badge a long time ago." He shot a stern look in Tessa's direction. "I didn't kill anybody, since I know that's what you're going to want to ask me. James wasn't any kind of hero, though. He knew what he was doing when he started to fence in the creek. There are people around here that depend on that water source. It would have made accessing the water so much harder, almost impossible. Not only that, but he built the fence a few feet onto my property, and tried to claim that it was his. My neighbor Pat and I were going to work together and try to sue James to stop him from building the fence."

"Pat?" Tessa raised her eyebrows. "He's such a quiet man, I'm surprised that he would get involved in something like that."

"He may be quiet, but he knows right from wrong. When I explained to him what was happening, he was more than happy to help me. I don't have the funds to hire a lawyer, so he agreed to team up with me to force James to stop building the fence." Kent's tone softened as he looked down at his feet. "I guess we don't have to worry about that anymore." He looked back up at Tessa. "I had nothing to do with this, Tessa, no matter what you suspect. I was handling things legally, I'm not a violent person."

"I don't doubt that for a second, Kent." Tessa frowned. "But isn't it possible that someone else is?"

"Who? Pat?" Kent shook his head. "He couldn't hurt a fly. He doesn't even kill the mosquitoes in the summer. He says it's his job to keep covered up."

"What about anyone else in the area? Maybe not someone upset about the fence, but upset about something else?" Tessa frowned. "I'm sure his business-first attitude ruffled some feathers around here."

"It did, but if you expect me to point out one of my neighbors and accuse them of murder, it's not going to happen." Kent crossed his arms as he stared at her. "Some of us understand loyalty."

"Loyalty for each other, but not for James, because he was an outsider right?" Cassie pushed her hair back over her shoulder as she gained Kent's attention. "Like me?"

"Cassie, don't take it personally, but most people around here have a lot more invested in their land than just money. They have memories, heritage, the kind of sentimental value that you can't get back. So yes, we do our best to protect each other and our community from losing that. It's just the way it is here." Kent let his arms fall back to his sides as he met her eyes. "It's why Sebastian is always at your place helping out. Because, he's your neighbor. We take care of each other."

"James was your neighbor, I don't see anyone interested in helping him, or the family he left behind." Tessa's voice hardened slightly.

"He wasn't neighborly." Kent scuffed his foot across the porch and shrugged. "If he wanted to be part of Little Leaf Creek, he wouldn't have insisted on building that fence in the first place."

"Well, it's not a problem for you anymore." Tessa frowned as she turned back toward the steps that led off of the porch.

Kent stared after her.

Cassie felt as if she could cut through the tension between the two as she followed after Tessa. When Tessa paused beside her jeep, she caught her by the arm.

"Tessa, why didn't you tell me you were coming out here?"

"Oh?" Tessa looked into her eyes. "Did my invitation to join you on this excursion get lost in the mail somehow?"

"I just happened to be driving by." Cassie's cheeks grew hot.

"After you went to the historical society?" Tessa smiled.

"I didn't think you would want to come with." Cassie shrugged. "We should work together. Like we have before. I was thinking about going by to talk to Zach." She tipped her head toward her car. "We could ride together." She explained what she had found out at the historical society.

"You go on to Zach. He isn't that fond of me. Besides, I already know that he didn't do it." Tessa opened the door to her jeep.

"What? How? Did you discover something?" Cassie watched as Tessa settled into her jeep.

"Sure did. My instincts. It's never the first person you suspect. Zach, he might have had motive and opportunity, but it's just too easy, isn't it?"

"I guess." Cassie frowned. "But I still want to check into him."

"You do that. I'll finish talking to the neighbors, and when we're done, we can compare notes. We still have a pie to bake you know." Tessa pulled the door shut and started the engine.

Cassie watched her drive off with an unsettled feeling. Had she offended Tessa by not inviting her along that morning? They had investigated murders together before, but it didn't occur to her to ask her to come to the historical society. Cassie knew that the cop Tessa once was, couldn't resist trying to solve the crime.

CHAPTER 12

After Cassie left Kent's, she headed down the road toward Zach's property. To her surprise she spotted an open sign hanging on his roadside stand. She had guessed that he would stay closed for the day, considering that a murder had taken place next door, and from what she understood he was a suspect. She parked close to the stand, then stepped out of the car. A tall lanky man stood at the back of the stand, his focus on the phone in his hand.

"How are you, Zach?"

"Huh?" Zach glanced up from his phone, then shook his head. "Sorry, trying to keep track of a lot of things today."

"That's alright. I'll just take a look around." Cassie

began to look through the assortment of produce. Although baskets of apples were featured prominently in the display, the various colors and shapes of the other fruit drew her attention. He sold everything from pale green pears, to vivid yellow lemons and bright orange mandarins. She allowed herself to be taken in by the beauty of the fruit for a moment, just a single second of not thinking about murder. When she glanced up at Zach again, all of it returned. Could this unassuming man have killed his neighbor? Could he have gone from cultivating such vibrant produce, to destroying life?

"Finding what you need?" Zach slipped his phone into his pocket.

"Yes, thank you." Cassie paused in front of him. "I came by on Monday to buy some apples, but you were closed."

"Yes, I closed early that day." Zach frowned. "I had a family emergency."

"Oh, I'm so sorry to hear that. Is everything okay?" Cassie piled some pears and mandarins on the counter near the register.

"Yes, it turned out to be a misunderstanding, actually." Zach shook his head. "My sister thought her son was missing. He hadn't come home from school when he was supposed to. She was in a panic, so I panicked, too, and went over there to try to help her find him. The kid was holed up in his tree house and had fallen asleep. By the time I got back here, the whole street was shut down."

"That must have been so scary for both of you. I'm glad he turned up. Was the street shut down because of the murder?" Cassie noticed the calmness in his voice as he spoke of his missing nephew.

Zach met her eyes. "Yes, because of that."

"You must have been so frightened. Maybe that family emergency was a stroke of luck. If you had been here, you could have been a target, too." Cassie pulled her wallet out of her purse.

"Oh, I doubt that." Zach began to ring up the fruit.

"No?" Cassie read the total on the cash register and handed him the money. "You don't think it was random? You think someone targeted James?"

"James had a lot of enemies." Zach handed her back some change. "He wasn't exactly kind to people."

"Including you?" Cassie narrowed her eyes. "I've heard he was trying to drive you out of business."

"Sure, he was trying." Zach shook out a paper bag, then began filling it with the fruit she purchased. "He even came over here one day to speak to me in person. He wanted to make sure that I understood it was nothing personal, it was just business." He rolled his eyes. "Just business."

"It sounds like it was pretty personal to me." Cassie took the bag from him.

"Of course it was. This is all I have." Zach gestured to his orchard. "He was determined to take it from me. I understand that because of his greed, now I'm the main suspect in his murder." He frowned as he met her eyes. "You're the first person who has come to my stand today. Usually, I'm almost sold out by now."

"Honestly, I didn't think that you would be open, after what happened."

"Maybe I shouldn't be, since no one is coming here to buy anything." Zach glanced at his phone again. "I've been trying to get a lawyer lined up, but it seems none of them want to take my case."

"I'm sorry to hear that." Cassie's heart skipped a beat. If even lawyers didn't want to take his case, then what did that say about him and his innocence? "You said James came over here to speak to you in person and tell you it was just business, how did that conversation end?"

"You mean, did I threaten to kill him and then follow through with it?" Zach looked back at her, his expression dark, and his tone sharp as he continued. "I guess you want some fresh gossip to take back to your friends?"

"I didn't mean it like that, Zach." Cassie took a sharp breath and a step back from him. "I just wondered how you left things between the two of you."

"The same way I'm going to leave it between us. I told him to get off my property, and never speak to me again!" Zach pointed to her car.

She started to turn away, but it wasn't fast enough.

"I said go!" Zach's shout snapped through her senses, setting off warning bells that made her heart race.

Cassie shuddered as she hurried back to her car. Sebastian had indicated that Zach was a good guy, but did he really know him?

Cassie stared at Zach through the windshield as she started her car.

Zach stared right back at her, his lips tight and his eyes narrowed.

Perhaps Cassie had pushed him a little too far with that last question. She guessed that Tessa would have been more subtle about things. She pulled away from the stand, onto the road, still a little shaken from the encounter. She'd arrived at the stand fairly convinced that although Zach had all the motive and opportunity he needed, he was likely not the killer. As she drove down the road, her opinion shifted. He had quite a temper. His alibi was a family emergency that turned out to be a misunderstanding. If his sister cared enough about him, she could easily have made up the alibi to protect him, once he confessed to her that he had killed a man.

Cassie didn't have any siblings herself, but she guessed that if she did, she would want to protect them. Would she lie to the police? Her heart pounded as she considered it. She'd lied about a lot of things when her husband was alive, mostly about how happy she was in the marriage. It didn't take much pressure to turn someone into a liar.

Before she could think further on it, bright flashing lights in her rearview mirror stole her attention.

CHAPTER 13

Cassie winced as the car with police lights and sirens blaring behind her edged closer. The initial fear of getting a ticket faded as she recognized the car, and the driver.

"Great." She sighed as she pulled over to the side of the road.

Oliver sat in his car for a few moments, then popped his door open.

Cassie tightened her grip on the steering wheel as she watched Oliver approach the car through her side mirror. No question that the man could wear a suit. He filled it out, not just with his fit frame, but with his arrogant attitude. She'd seen his softer side, but that wasn't enough to erase the edge of authority he wore as sharp and shiny as the badge he wore.

"Cassie." He stretched one arm along the top of her car and leaned down to look through her window. "What are you doing out here?"

"Was I speeding, Detective?" Cassie looked straight into his eyes.

"Since these roads don't have an official speed limit, I'm going to have to say no." Oliver quirked an eyebrow as he looked past her, to the pile of produce on the seat beside her. "Doing a little shopping today?"

"Oliver, I don't have time for this." Cassie frowned.

"It won't take long. Didn't I tell you to be cautious of everyone? You have to know that Zach is a suspect." Oliver crouched down beside the car so he could look her straight in the eyes. "Didn't I warn you that you could be in danger if the killer suspected that you saw something incriminating?"

"Yes, and yes." Cassie frowned as she realized the whole reason for this charade. "Ollie, I was fine. I just wanted to see how he was doing. Did he tell you that story about his nephew?"

"Yes, he did, and his sister backed him up." Oliver tilted his head to the side. "Of course that doesn't mean much of anything, because she could easily be lying. Neither of them filed a police report that stated the boy was missing."

"I guess they found him fast enough that they didn't have to." Cassie sat back against the seat of the car and closed her eyes. "However, I didn't hear any panic in Zach's voice when he talked about his nephew being missing. Yes, he's been found now, but if he had been missing, I'd guess there would be a little leftover fear." She paused as she wondered if she should reveal Zach's demands for her to leave. She didn't want to give Oliver the wrong impression. It wasn't as if Zach had put his hands on her, and she had asked him questions about the murder which aggravated him.

"Cassie, being alone with him, it's just not the best decision. I can't do my job, if I'm having to look out for you." Oliver straightened up. "I'd hope that you would have enough common sense not to put yourself in that kind of dangerous situation."

Oliver's implied insult wasn't lost on her as she stared through the open window at him. "I'm fine, aren't I? I guess I wasn't at risk after all."

"Just do me a favor, try to stay out of this. I'm doing my best to work through this investigation, I can't be worried about you the whole time." Oliver stepped back from the car.

"I'm not asking you to be worried about me." Cassie tightened her grip on the steering wheel. "In fact, I don't think you should be. I'm perfectly capable of protecting myself."

"Oh?" Oliver nodded. "Alright then. Carry on."

As Oliver turned and walked back toward his car she wondered if she should call him back and apologize for her harsh tone. But she meant it. She liked him as a friend, but his determination to make decisions for her, left her with a bad taste in her mouth. Maybe it was his nature, maybe it was just his time on the job, either way, she didn't want to be told what to do. She had played inside the lines for so long that she forgot there was a world outside of them. She never wanted to be back in that situation again. Just as she was about to turn the key in the ignition, he stepped back up to the window.

"Listen, I get it, you think I'm trying to tell you what to do." Oliver crossed his arms.

"I didn't say that."

"You don't have to say it. But you need to be careful. You can't afford to place yourself at risk." Oliver rested his hands on the window as he looked in at her. "So, you can accuse me of being too concerned, or you can tell me to leave you alone, but that's not going to change my attitude about any of this. You're my friend, Cassie, and I'm going to do what I can to keep you safe, whether you like it or not."

Startled by the intensity of Oliver's words, and the determined stare that continued to pin her to her seat, she searched for a moment for the right response.

"Thank you."

"You're welcome." Oliver smiled, then straightened up. "Speaking of friends, I noticed Sebastian's truck outside of your house."

"Oh no!" Cassie winced as she recalled their plans to work on the house.

"See, you have enough on your plate, Cassie, leave the investigating to me." Oliver nodded to her, then strode back to his car.

Cassie started her car, and continued down the road, still a bit unsettled by their conversation. He had been there the moment she needed him, and he did always seem to have her safety in mind. She loved that he had declared her his friend, but she hoped that didn't mean that he intended to get in her way of investigating the murder. She had to know what happened to James, not just for the sake of his family, but for herself as well. Had she been there moments sooner, what would she have seen? Who would she have caught in the act?

Cassie's mind spun as she sped up to get to her house. He was right, she did have a lot of things on her plate, between working at the diner, trying to fix up her house, and hoping to pull off a great holiday meal, but she also wanted to help find James' murderer so she could put it to rest.

CHAPTER 14

Cassie sighed as she spotted Sebastian sitting on the rocking chair on her front porch.

"I'm sorry!" She climbed out of her car and waved to him as she approached.

"Keeping me waiting, as usual." Sebastian rocked all the way forward in the chair as he peered at her. "Should I be taking this personally?"

"Sebastian, I really am so, so, sorry." Cassie sighed as she reached the top step of the porch. "I got caught up in things, and lost track of time."

"What things?" Sebastian stood up and stretched his arms above his head. "Wild horses? Wandering babies? What could be more important than slapping a few coats of paint on your walls with me?"

"I stopped by Zach's stand." Cassie set the paper bags down on the empty rocking chair.

"Oh." Sebastian eyed the bags, then looked back at her. "Did you talk to him?"

"Yes." Cassie pushed her hair behind her shoulders.

"You sure are the curious type, aren't you?" Sebastian smiled some. "Can't leave anything alone?"

"Do you think I should?" Cassie's muscles tensed at the thought of another lecture about her staying out of things.

"Not at all." Sebastian held a paint brush out to her. "I think you should tell me all about it, while we get to work. What did Zach have to say for himself?"

As Cassie shared with him her encounter with both Kent and Zach, she decided to leave out her run-in with Oliver. When she described Zach's reaction to her, he dropped his paintbrush into the pan and turned to face her.

"Zach lost his temper with you?"

"Not exactly." Cassie noticed the hardness in Sebastian's voice. "He just seemed very frustrated."

"I can't blame him for that, but that's no excuse for frightening you."

"You really don't think he did this?" Cassie searched his eyes. "How can you be so sure?"

"I can't be completely sure. But I just don't believe it. I know Zach. He's a good man. He wouldn't hurt anyone." Sebastian hesitated, then frowned. "Although, I'm sorry that he treated you the way that he did."

"It's alright." Cassie studied him for a moment and wondered if his loyalty to his friend had blinded him to some of Zach's flaws.

Sebastian picked up his paintbrush and went back to work, though his strokes were sharper than before.

Cassie considered asking him more questions about Zach, but from his change in demeanor she guessed that it wasn't a good idea. Since she had left him waiting, she didn't want to ruffle his feathers any further. Instead, she turned her focus on the task at hand. She began to paint around the front windows. With each stroke of the paintbrush, her mind ran through another suspect. She started with Zach, and ended with Ben's two children. As she sorted through them, she began to hum, a trick that helped her to concentrate while multi-tasking. It was something she hadn't even noticed until she was married and her husband pointed it out, as a rather irritating behavior.

Again, she didn't notice as she continued to paint, until Sebastian's rich, smooth voice began to sing the words to the song she hummed. He did so softly at first, but the more he sang, the louder his voice became.

Cassie blushed as she realized she'd been humming, then gave a short laugh. "Let me guess, you were in the church choir?"

"You know me too well." Sebastian grinned as he set his paintbrush down in a nearly empty paint pan."

"Sorry about the humming, it's a habit, I don't even notice it." Cassie set her brush down as well.

"Don't apologize, it's wonderful. I just couldn't help singing along." Sebastian stretched his arms out and gave a short growl. "We've gotten a lot done so far."

"Maybe it's a good time to break for an afternoon snack?" Cassie winced as her stomach rumbled. "Actually, I don't think I ever had lunch."

"We can't have that. I can throw together a fruit salad with some of the produce you bought." Sebastian grabbed the paper bags that never made it into the house.

"Sebastian, you can't paint my house and make me lunch. What will the neighbors think?" Cassie grinned as she followed him into the house.

"Hopefully they'll think, that Sebastian really knows how to romance a lady." Sebastian dropped the bags on the kitchen counter and turned to face her.

As his eyes met hers, her heart raced. Did that sly smile on his lips indicate that his words were a joke, or was he waiting for a reaction from her?

"I'm sure the neighbors have plenty of wonderful things to think about you." Cassie edged around him to the refrigerator to gather the rest of the ingredients for the salad. "And I totally agree. You've been so kind to me since I moved here, Sebastian, I can't thank you enough for that."

"But you can avoid the topic." Sebastian grabbed a knife from a drawer and began to slice up one of the pears.

Sebastian's words hung between them as she realized he wasn't going to let her laugh off his flirtation this time and change the subject. So far, their game of him piling compliments on her, and her habit of dismissing his flirty comments as just part of his charm, had kept them away from any awkward conversations. It still was hard for her to believe that he was interested in her, but then, she'd never been good at picking up on those kinds of things. She'd been attracted to both Sebastian and Oliver since she'd moved to Little Leaf Creek, as well as an even stronger determination to stay away from romance.

Sebastian set a piece of watermelon next to the cutting board then continued to slice the pears, his words still adding pressure to the air between them.

The easy thing would be to crack a joke, and move on. Sebastian would let her, she knew that. He was respectful to a fault, and didn't ever make her feel uncomfortable or pinned down. Her mind jumped to Tessa, who had spent so much of her life alone. Cassie had assumed that after her husband died, she would do the same. But she'd spent most of her life in a loveless marriage, did she really want to spend the rest of her life alone? Her husband's death at a young age had sharpened her perspective on things. A long life was never guaranteed.

"Got any more orange juice?"

Sebastian's voice interrupted her thoughts. Flustered, she shook her head. "No sorry."

"That's alright, it'll still be tasty." Sebastian set the knife down and tossed the pear slices into the large bowl she provided. "Did I scare you off?"

"Scare me off?" Cassie began to peel the mandarins.

"You went quiet on me." Sebastian began to slice the watermelon.

"I'm sorry, I'm just a little distracted."

"Then maybe this isn't the best time for me to bring up the concert I want to take you to?" Sebastian tossed the watermelon into the bowl.

"Concert?" Cassie looked up at him.

"There is a band from Freemar that's pretty good. I think you'll like it. It's playing this weekend. I picked up a couple of tickets." Sebastian took a deep breath, his cheeks flushed, and he looked her straight in the eyes. "Would you like to join me? I know it's a little last minute, but the tickets were sold out, then a few became available, and I snatched them up. I can go alone, but I'd much rather go with you."

"I'm sure there are plenty of other people you can invite." Cassie's heart pounded as she realized that going to a concert together was definitely a date. Wasn't it?

"I'm not inviting anyone else." Sebastian stepped closer to her, his eyes still locked to hers. "I bought the tickets because I want to go with you. It's up to you if you don't want to, but I want to be clear with you, Cassie. I'd really like to take you out, and if you give me a chance, I think we'd both have a great time."

CHAPTER 15

Cassie held her breath as her heart slammed against her chest. This was it, this was the moment when she had to decide whether she ever wanted to open herself up to romance again. It was just a concert, just a friendly date, but it was exactly what she had planned to avoid. In fact, since she had agreed to go out with Oliver and then that fell through and they had decided to be friends, she was even more determined to remain single. So, why did she have such an urge to say yes?

The sharp blare of a horn distracted her before she could make a decision.

"Who's that?" Sebastian's eyes narrowed as he looked out through the screen door. "It's Ollie." He sighed.

"I should see what he wants, it must be important." Cassie hurried past him, and through the door.

Though Sebastian didn't say a word, she sensed his frustration as he followed a few steps behind her.

Oliver stepped out of his car and rounded it, toward the front gate.

"I need to speak with you, Cassie."

"Is something wrong?" Cassie noticed the tension in his features and the tight tone of his voice as she opened the gate for him.

"I don't know how many different ways I can tell you to stay out of this." Oliver frowned as he looked straight into her eyes. "This is an official murder investigation, every time you go stirring things up, you put yourself in danger. By questioning James' neighbors, you could make someone come after you."

"I only spoke with Zach, which we already spoke about, and Kent." Cassie took a slight step back. "Tessa was there with me."

"Yes, I know." Oliver crossed his arms as he looked toward Tessa's house. "I'll be speaking with her, too, but she's not home." He turned his attention back to Cassie. "So, you're the one that I'm going to start with."

"Ollie, I'm sorry, I didn't mean to cross any lines." Cassie wondered what Tessa might have found out from the other neighbors, but Oliver's flushed cheeks brought her focus back to him. "I didn't think I was causing any harm."

"You were at the scene of the crime, the killer might have seen you, and yet you keep going around putting yourself in danger. Do you think I have nothing else to do other than to make sure you're okay?" Oliver's cheeks flushed as he drew his lips into a tight line.

"Ollie!" Sebastian stepped up beside Cassie and glared at the other man.

"I've never asked you to do that." Cassie's temper began to flare, as she felt humiliated by his lecture. "I'm perfectly capable of assessing and taking my own risks, Ollie. I'm not sure what makes you think I'm not."

"If those risks you decide to take continue to interfere with my investigation, then we are going to have a problem." Oliver looked from her to Sebastian, then back again. "This is between you and me, no one else."

"Why not just tell her the truth, Ollie?" Sebastian rolled his eyes. "You're just upset because people are giving her and Tessa more information than they are giving you."

"Why not just stay out of this, Sebastian?" Oliver looked at him. "This is between Cassie and me."

"It's understandable that they might tell us more. Some people don't like talking to the police." Cassie smiled slightly.

"Probably because they have already told you and Tessa everything." Oliver shook his head.

"Instead of blaming Cassie, why don't you just ask her what she found out?" Sebastian put his hand on Cassie's shoulder.

"If there's anything I should know, I hope you'll share it with me." Oliver avoided looking at Sebastian.

"Of course I will. I told you about Zach." Cassie frowned. "Ollie, I didn't mean to interfere, if anything, I just want to help."

"Just be careful." Oliver straightened up and took a step back.

"I will be." Cassie nodded. "I'm sure that you'll get to the truth. Don't take my curiosity as lack of faith in you."

"I'm trying not to." Oliver nodded to her, then turned and stepped through the gate to his car.

Cassie watched as he pulled away.

She turned back to the house just in time to see Sebastian step out. She wanted to ask him about the tension between him and Oliver. Tessa had said that it was because they were both vying for Cassie's affections, but she wasn't sure. What would they see in her?

"I think we've done enough for today." Sebastian tugged his cap down over his blond hair and looked toward the cans of paint. "Let me help you clean this up, then I'll be on my way."

"Don't you want to have the salad?" Cassie stepped up onto the porch.

"No, thanks." Sebastian walked toward the paint cans. "I'm not feeling that hungry anymore. You enjoy it."

Although Sebastian's tone remained pleasant, his demeanor had shifted. He stood with his back to her, he avoided her eyes, and didn't invite any further conversation.

"Okay, as long as you're sure." Cassie pointed toward the pans. "Don't worry about that, I can clean it up." She brushed her hair back over her shoulders as she looked at him. Since the interruption, he hadn't mentioned the concert. She hadn't agreed to go with him. Maybe she'd said something that had made him think twice about the invitation.

"Alright, I'll see you tomorrow then." Sebastian nodded to her, then headed down the steps in the direction of his truck.

Cassie was tempted to call out to him, to tell him that she'd be happy to go to the concert with him, but decided against it. She had enough mysteries on her plate. She didn't need to dive into the mystery of her romantic life on top of it all. She was just about to step back inside the house when she heard a car door slam in the driveway next door. The moment she spotted Tessa, she headed right over.

CHAPTER 16

"Tessa, did you talk with the other neighbors?" Cassie followed her up the steps to her front porch.

"Sure I did." Tessa opened the door, then crouched down to greet Harry. "Actually, only one. Pat." She looked up at her. "I wanted to see if what he had to say would match what Kent had to say."

"And did it?" Cassie's eyes narrowed.

"Mostly, yes. But it's pretty clear to me that Pat got pulled into this whole mess. Kent is the one that actually has the biggest problem with the fence. Pat has deep pockets and the right contacts to stir up trouble. But he hated the idea of going against his neighbor. Kent is the one who pushed for it."

"I see." Cassie shook her head. "It sounds like Kent had quite an ax to grind."

"Come inside, we still have a pie to bake." Tessa led the way and turned on the oven. "I rolled out the crust already. It takes a while to roll."

"I had a bit of a run-in with Oliver." Cassie stepped up beside Tessa as Tessa retrieved the pie crust and cooked apples from the fridge.

"Shocking." Tessa gave a short laugh. "He is quite preoccupied by you, isn't he? What ever happened on your date?"

"We decided to be friends. Although, that may change since I can't stop stepping on his toes." Cassie watched as Tessa poured some rice onto the parchment paper that sat on top of the pie crust, then slipped it into the oven. "Don't we want to add in the apples?"

"It's good to let the crust crisp a bit first, that way the pastry will cook through and the apples won't make it too soggy." Tessa closed the oven door, then turned to face Cassie. "I think we need to figure out what exactly James was up to. People don't just get killed out of the blue, most of the time. Usually, there's a reason. They've gotten themselves into some kind of trouble, or crossed the wrong person. I'm going to dig a bit into his financial situation.

From what I understand, he had a strange deal going with Ben's children. Maybe there's a reason for that. Maybe he didn't have the funds he pretended to."

"He had to have something. He was selling his produce so cheap that he couldn't be turning a profit on it." Cassie sniffed the air as the scent of the cinnamon in the crust wafted through it.

"Exactly." Tessa snapped her fingers. "Which is why we need to dig deeper. My guess is that James had quite a few secrets of his own."

"You're absolutely right. But with him only living here for a short time, it might be hard to find out any solid information." Cassie frowned.

"Don't worry, I have lots of connections." Tessa smiled. "I think the crust is ready." She slipped on an oven mitt and pulled open the door to the oven. "Yes, it smells done."

"It smells delicious." Cassie closed her eyes and savored the scent for a moment. Memories of past Thanksgivings flooded through her. When she opened them again, she felt a fresh determination to make Thanksgiving happen. "So, you add in the apples, now?"

"I like to have a taste and add a bit more spice when I do." Tessa tasted the filling. "My apple pies have quite a kick."

"I can't wait to taste it." Cassie smiled. "And find out what your secret ingredient is."

"Good luck! Now, for the artwork." Tessa began laying the pastry over the top of the filling to make a lattice top. Cassie was shocked at how simple she made it look and how relaxed she looked while she was making it. "Brush the egg over."

"That's something I can do." Cassie smiled as she painted the beaten egg over the top of the pastry.

Tessa slid the pie back into the oven.

"Well, we have some time to wait." Tessa sat down at the table. "What do you say we think this through a bit?"

"I brought my notebook." Cassie settled at the table across from her. "Maybe it would be a good idea to go over the suspects that we have so far."

"Zach, of course." Tessa nodded.

"Yes, he's on the top of the list, with the evidence we have so far. But I definitely think that Ben's kids might have been involved. Maybe they felt as if James was betraying their father's memory and reputation."

"Maybe." Tessa tapped her chin. "Don't forget Kent, and Pat. The two of them felt a little off to me."

"Yes, good point. Then there are the three workers that were actually at the orchard when

James was killed. I still find it hard to believe that none of them saw anything suspicious. But the orchard is large. I guess it's possible." Cassie jotted down their names. "I don't know if any of them were involved, but I suspect that at least one of them knows more than they are saying."

"It's hard to believe that anyone would attack the person that's employing them, though." Tessa sighed. "Jobs aren't always easy to come by around here. But Colin worked with Ben since the start, he even worked with Ben's dad before Ben took over, so there must have been some loyalty there."

"There's also the ex-employees, including Duncan's father, Nathan." Cassie jotted down his name at the bottom of the list. "It's hard to believe that one orchard can impact so many people in such a small town."

"We are a true community, when one cog breaks down, the whole town feels it." Tessa smiled some.

"If it's such a close community, then why do you keep yourself so far from it, Tessa?" Cassie frowned as she looked up at her.

"Sometimes people aren't lonely because they're alone, Cassie. Sometimes they're alone because they chose to be, because it's easier that way." Tessa winked at her. "I have my small circle, and I like it that way. Not so many slices of pie to share, which means more for me."

Cassie obliged her with a smile, but she sensed Tessa was hiding the truth beneath her lighthearted tone. She couldn't imagine anyone preferring to be alone all of the time. Although, she enjoyed spending some time alone. Though she'd often imagined her life as a single woman while she was still married, she'd always been a little frightened by the idea. Having a warm smile to greet her meant a lot to her.

"I'm grateful to be part of your circle, Tessa." Cassie gave her hand a light pat.

"Good, that means you can have some pie." Tessa laughed as she stood back up and retrieved the pie from the oven. "We'll have to let it cool a bit, then you can have the first slice."

Harry whimpered from underneath the table.

"Now Harry, Cassie is our guest."

"I'd love to have that first piece, Tessa, but I actually have to go." Cassie winced as she looked at the clock. "I'm due at the diner for my shift." She shook her head as she stood up. "I feel like I'm always running behind these days." She sniffed the air over the pie and groaned. "That is probably the best thing that I have ever smelled."

"It might be." Tessa grinned. "How about I bring you a slice of pie to the diner when it's ready?"

"You'd do that?" Cassie's eyes widened. "But it'll be in the middle of dinner rush."

"That's alright, it'll give the locals something to gossip about." Tessa grinned.

"Thanks so much, Tessa!" Cassie hurried out the door and back to her house to collect her things. As she tugged her hair into a ponytail she recalled Sebastian's invitation. For a moment she considered sending him a text to accept it. But what if the moment had passed? Was it too late for her to reach out now?

With Sebastian still on her mind, Cassie settled into her shift at the diner.

With so many questions floating through her mind about Sebastian and the murder, Cassie found it hard to concentrate as she served the customers who came and left. She did her best to focus, but she mixed up a few orders, and endured some complaints from the diners. Each time she received one, she glanced over at Mirabel, who met her eyes, then looked away. She wanted the job, that was for sure, but she wondered how many mistakes it would take before Mirabel decided that she was more trouble than she was worth.

Feeling frustrated, Cassie did her best to clear

her thoughts. After a few minutes of keeping herself calm, she began to get into the swing of the routine. Everything went much smoother.

Until, she noticed Tessa waving to her through the window of the diner.

Cassie waved back, pointed to her watch and indicated she'd be out in a few minutes.

Tessa nodded.

Once Cassie had made sure that all of her tables had everything they needed, she sent a guilty glance in Mirabel's direction, but she was busy with the customers at the counter. She hurried to the door and stepped out to greet Tessa.

"Hi Tessa. Sorry, I had to take care of a few tables."

"That's okay. It's a bit too crowded in there for me. But I brought you a slice of pie." Tessa held up a small container.

"Thank you so much for bringing me the pie, but it really is busy in there." Cassie took the container that Tessa offered her.

"It sure looks like it. Good luck!" Tessa started to walk back to her car.

"Tessa wait! Are you sure you don't want to come in for a cup of coffee or something? I can make it for you. It should get quiet in about fifteen minutes, I might get a chance to sit and eat the pie with you." Cassie held open the door for her.

"I don't know." Tessa stared through the door at the crowd of people.

"Don't worry, it's not as bad as it looks, most people are finishing up their meals." Cassie tipped her head toward the counter. "See? The counter is already starting to clear out."

"I guess, just for a few minutes." Tessa made her way inside.

"Cassie, table twelve!" Mirabel shouted to her from behind the counter.

"On it!" Cassie hurried over to the frustrated diners who had been waiting on her.

"Tessa?" Mirabel smiled, as she patted an empty spot on the counter. "Come sit, I'll get you some coffee."

Relieved that Tessa would be taken care of, Cassie apologized to the diners, then made up for her absence with smiles and as much extra attention as she could manage. By the time she had a chance to sit down next to Tessa, her legs ached from all of the running around.

"Tell me again why you do this to yourself?" Tessa sipped her coffee as she looked at her.

"It's a good job." Cassie ignored her burning feet

and took a bite of the apple pie. "Tessa!" She gasped as the flavors danced along the surface of her tongue. "This is amazing!"

"I bet it is." Mirabel leaned against the counter. "I've been hearing about Tessa's apple pie for years. But I've never had a taste myself."

"Not a chance, Mirabel." Tessa eyed her. "One bite, and you'll figure out my secret, and soon enough you'll be selling my pie to every hungry customer."

"Would that be so terrible? You never make it anymore." Mirabel shrugged, then winked at Cassie. "At least you didn't, until Cassie came to town."

Cassie smiled as she took another bite.

"I'm so glad she did. This is the best apple pie I've ever tasted."

"Yes well, I'm glad to see you enjoy it." Tessa finished the last sip of her coffee. "I'll be on my way." She left a few dollars on the counter and walked out of the diner.

"Well, she seems to have warmed up to you." Mirabel smiled. "She seems much happier. You're really good for her."

"I hope so." Cassie smiled at the thought. She pushed over the rest of the pie and handed a fork to Mirabel. "I know she's really good for me, not so much for my waistline, though. I just hope that I can coax her into having Thanksgiving dinner."

"Good luck." Mirabel grinned as she picked up a forkful of pie. "You're going to need it. With Tessa, and with that table that's still waiting for their check."

"Oh no!" Cassie jumped back to her feet.

CHAPTER 18

Finally, things began to calm down again. Just as Cassie thought she would have a rest, the door swung open. As she looked up at the door she caught sight of a face she recognized. Colin, one of the three men that had been at the orchard when Cassie had found James' body, walked toward a table. Another man followed just behind him, one she didn't recognize. As they settled at a table she started toward them to take their order, but found Mirabel was there first with her order pad out.

Surprised, as it was not very busy, Cassie busied herself wiping down the counter. After a short conversation, Colin laughed, shook his head, then shooed Mirabel away.

Mirabel's smile faded as she turned toward Cassie.

"What was that about?" Cassie met her eyes as she stepped behind the counter.

"I didn't want you to take their table." Mirabel began filling glasses of water for the two men. "You'll get too busy questioning them to actually serve them." She tipped her head toward the table. "That's Duncan's father, Nathan, with Colin."

"Oh!" Cassie felt a sudden urge to rush right over to the table and question him, just as Mirabel had predicted. She resisted the urge and frowned. "I'm sorry, Mirabel, I guess I haven't been a very good waitress lately."

"Don't be sorry, just don't cause any drama." Mirabel gave her a light pat on the shoulder. "And you're a good waitress, Cassie, just a little distracted."

Cassie felt some relief at Mirabel's response, but her attention shifted right back to Colin and Nathan. The two men leaned close to each other, their voices low. If she had any hope of hearing what they were discussing she needed to get closer. Luckily, a woman walked into the diner just then.

"Hi, welcome to Mirabel's." Cassie flashed her a smile as she stepped out from behind the counter, which put her in earshot of Colin's table. "How many?" She grabbed a menu.

"Just me. The counter's fine." The woman laughed as she sat down on one of the stools.

Disappointed, Cassie strained to hear what she could of the men's discussion.

"I told you, Colin, I wasn't anywhere near the orchard that day. I told the police that, too. I don't know why you keep asking me. You were the one that was there."

"I didn't do it." Colin shot his words back in a sharper tone.

"I didn't say you did."

"Uh, coffee please?" The woman at the counter waved her hand in front of Cassie's face.

"Sure, sorry." Cassie shook her head. "I've been a little spacey these days." She walked around behind the counter and prepared the woman a cup of coffee.

"I understand, I've been running in circles all day myself. I've been trying to get a clear read on what happened out at that orchard, and it seems to me that everyone has a different idea about it." She settled her gaze on Cassie. "Which is why I came here to talk to you."

"Me?" Cassie set the coffee down in front of her. "Who are you?" As she studied the young woman's features she couldn't recall seeing her before.

"Jocelyn." She held out her hand. "Jocelyn Stafford. I'm a reporter, from Highcrest."

"Highcrest?" Cassie took the woman's hand in a brief shake. "Isn't that over an hour away?"

"It is, but news has been slow, and I'm hoping to score a feature story from covering this murder." Jocelyn sighed as she picked up her cup of coffee. "But I can't do that without some kind of genuine information."

"Funny, I find myself needing some information, too." Cassie eyed the woman. "Maybe we could help each other?"

"Are you a reporter, too?" Jocelyn laughed.

"No, just curious enough to be one. I've been hoping to get in touch with the former owner's family." Cassie lowered her voice. "I'll tell you what I saw, if you can get me that information."

"Oh, you mean you want to talk to Bethany and Noah?" Jocelyn pulled her phone out of her purse. "Sure, I have Bethany's contact information." She jotted it down on the back of a business card and passed it across the counter to her. "Good luck, I haven't been able to get through to anyone. Why do you want to talk to them?"

"I suppose I'd just like to see how they're doing. I know they're caught in the middle of this tragedy." Cassie frowned.

"Not sure what you can do for them at this point. Bethany's still pretty devastated over the loss of her father."

"Maybe I can help in some way." Cassie slipped the card into her pocket. "I lost my husband not that long ago."

"I'm sorry to hear that." Jocelyn stared into Cassie's eyes. "Is that what brought you here? I've heard you're fairly new in town."

"It's part of it." Cassie nodded, as her mind rushed back to the days after her husband's death. He had been killed in a car accident. Rumor had spread that the car had been tampered with and that maybe she had arranged the accident to get the inheritance. All of the friends she thought she had, looked at her with accusing stares. It didn't matter that it was just rumors and an accident. All that mattered was that she was too numb to cry, and his life insurance would make her a wealthy woman. So, they thought she was guilty. She pushed the memories away and took another breath. "I'd just like to check in with them."

"Now, you can." Jocelyn smiled. "How about you

tell me about finding James?"

As Cassie recounted the experience, her heart fluttered with the recollection of James' body sprawled across the ground. She didn't go into too much detail. She didn't want to relive some aspects of the incident or upset those close to James.

"That must have been difficult for you." Jocelyn's voice softened. "Are you handling it alright?"

"Yes. Luckily, I have a few good friends here."

"I'm glad to hear that." Jocelyn tucked her phone into her pocket. "Thanks for the information. Give me a call if you think of anything else." She piled a few dollars on the counter, then turned and headed for the door.

Cassie looked back toward Colin's table and found it empty. She winced as she realized she'd missed her chance to speak to either of them, distracted by Jocelyn's questions. At least she'd gotten Bethany's number.

Cassie walked over to clean off their table and caught sight of another man who stepped in the door.

"Miah." His name popped out of her mouth.

"Cassie." Miah walked over to her. "How are you? I've been worried about you. Colin mentioned you were working, and I thought I'd check in with you."

"That's kind of you." Cassie gestured to the empty table. "Would you like to sit? I'll get you some coffee."

"Sure, thanks. But no coffee, a chocolate milkshake would be good. My nerves are still a little on edge after everything that happened." Miah settled in a chair. "But you still haven't told me how you are."

"Sorry." Cassie shook her head. "I'm still a little shaken up, but okay. I just can't stop thinking about who might have done this."

"Oh, I've heard all about you trying to snoop around." Miah raised an eyebrow. "I expect I'm next on your list to question?"

Cassie bit into the tip of her tongue to stop herself from admitting that he was right.

"I just spoke with a few neighbors after I'd heard that they had some problems with James. Have you heard anything about that?" Cassie cleared her throat.

"You mean Kent? Yes, I told the police about it, too. I think you're on the right track there." Miah narrowed his eyes. "I just can't believe this happened."

"What makes you so sure Kent was involved?" Cassie's heart pounded at the thought.

"I've seen him and Zach huddled together in that booth." Miah turned and pointed toward the window, then looked back at her. "I knew they were up to something, and I knew it had something to do with James, or at least I suspected it did when I saw the way they reacted when they saw me, but I had no idea they planned to kill him!"

"Did you ever hear them talking about the possibility?" Cassie looked toward the now empty booth, then looked back at him.

Cassie noticed a flicker of uncertainty cross Miah's features before he shook his head.

"No, not at all. But they were plenty angry at him. I can't blame Zach, he was losing everything. I think that's when he started drinking so much. When his wife found out the farm was about to go into foreclosure, she took the kids and moved to her mother's." Miah sighed. "And Kent, was so angry about that fence."

"Zach began drinking more than usual?" Cassie recalled his quick temper. How much quicker would it have been if he was also drunk?

"Much more. He didn't always make it home on his own. I've given him a lift a few times to make sure that he got home safe." Miah shook his head. "I've been out to his home a few times and he'd be on a rant, about money, or James, or the town. I did my best to calm him down. I knew he was drunk. When he's sober, he'd never treat his wife or the kids that way, not that that's an excuse. I'd convince him to leave for the night, stay in the barn until he could dry out, and that would be the end of it." He shook his head. "His wife never wanted to call the police."

"So, you're close to Zach?" Cassie looked into his eyes.

"Before James took over the orchard, Zach and I were good friends. But once James took over, things got a little tense between us. I don't know why. I mean, I have to work." Miah frowned. "I went out there to try and help him, but it was never the same."

"You're a good friend for making sure he was okay."

"Maybe if I'd been a better friend, he wouldn't be in this mess." Miah sighed and sat back in his chair. "I don't know. Maybe I could have done something."

"Don't put that on yourself. If Zach was involved in this, he is the only one that is responsible for it." Cassie smiled, then walked off to get his drink. As she did, she wondered if Miah was trying to divert the suspicion from himself by placing it on Zach and Kent.

CHAPTER 19

As Cassie worked the remainder of her shift, her thoughts danced between Zach and Kent. They were both losing out because of James' presence. Did the two of them work out some kind of plan to get rid of him? If so, how could she prove it? As she mulled over the idea of breaking into Zach's house to look for evidence, Oliver's voice popped up in her mind, warning her to be careful.

"No, that certainly wouldn't be very careful." Cassie sighed as she considered her options. Maybe she should go talk to Oliver first and see if he was willing to share any more information about the case. Maybe he had found out something about Zach or Kent. Maybe she could drop in with a sweet surprise and he'd be willing to forgive her for interfering. She doubted it, but it was worth a try.

"Headed out?" Mirabel glanced up at the large clock on the wall.

"If that's okay." Cassie lifted her apron off over her head and hung it on a hook.

"Yes, that's fine. Why don't you come in a bit late tomorrow?"

"Uh oh." Cassie frowned as she met Mirabel's eyes. "I'm sorry about being so distracted."

"It's okay, Cassie, but I really think you need to slow down a little bit, and process everything that happened. Alright?" Mirabel smiled. "Don't worry, you're not in any trouble with me."

"Does that mean I can make a milkshake to go?" Cassie walked over to the blender.

"Of course you can. Why do I get the feeling it's not for you?" Mirabel watched as Cassie piled in the ice cream.

"It's for Ollie."

"Sweets for your sweet?" Mirabel raised her eyebrows. "But what about poor Sebastian?"

"Ollie and I are just friends, or at least I hope we still will be, after all of this is over." Cassie added some milk.

"So, what does that make you and Sebastian?" Mirabel's voice took on a sing-song lilt.

"Oh, you're sneaky! That was a setup!" Cassie glared at Mirabel, then laughed. "We're just friends, too." She turned on the blender to drown out anything else Mirabel had to say.

Yes, just friends. It was for the best that she had never accepted the invitation to the concert. Mirabel was right about one thing, she did need to slow down. She needed to pay attention to the new life she'd started, instead of jumping ahead into a future that she wasn't ready for.

After greeting the officer at the front desk and asking to see Oliver, Cassie made her way to his office.

"I brought you a milkshake." Cassie smiled as she peeked around the corner of his open door. She walked in and set it down on his desk in front of him. "Think of it as a peace offering."

"I think I should be the one making the offering. After the way I've been acting." Oliver peered at the milkshake, then looked back up at her. "Is this a peace offering or a bribe?"

"You really are a great detective." Cassie sat down across from him. "Can we talk about Zach a little bit?"

"What about him?" Oliver took a sip of his milkshake.

"He's a suspect, isn't he?" Cassie leaned forward.

"Everyone is a suspect." Oliver frowned.

"Okay, so you don't want to tell me more." Cassie nodded. "I understand. I guess he must be, since he had motive and opportunity."

"Maybe. I hate thinking that someone living in Little Leaf Creek is capable of murder. But it's possible they are." Oliver set the milkshake down as he leaned forward. "Everyone thinks that working in such a small town is the easy way out when it comes to law enforcement, but the truth is, it's harder. No one is a stranger here. You played on the same baseball teams, you went to the same schools, you know their kids. It's not as simple as just making an arrest."

"I imagine not." Cassie nodded. "Do you think maybe Zach and Kent could be involved in this together?"

"It's possible. All I can say is to stay away from Zach. Stay away from Kent." Oliver stood up from his desk.

"What about Nathan? Duncan's father?"

"He's been eliminated as a suspect. He has a solid alibi." Oliver picked up his milkshake. "Thanks for the treat, Cassie." He walked around the side of his desk, then paused beside her. "Anyone could have done this. I hope that Zach and Kent aren't involved, but they might be. I am telling you this so you are cautious. Please stay out of this investigation, okay?"

"Okay." Cassie forced a smile but she had no intention of staying out of it.

As soon as Cassie had some coffee the next morning, she sat down with her phone, and dialed Bethany's number. She expected, as Jocelyn had predicted, that Bethany wouldn't answer. Instead, she heard a young woman's voice pick up on the second ring.

"Hello?"

"Hi, is this Bethany?" A bit startled that she answered, Cassie tried to gather her thoughts.

"Yes, who is this?" Bethany paused. "I'm expecting a call from someone. That's the only reason I answered."

"Oh, I see." Cassie took a breath. She guessed the only way she would get to the truth was to offer it first. "My name is Cassie. I moved to Little Leaf

Creek, recently. I happened to be at the property that used to belong to your father, shortly after James was killed. I found him." She braced herself for the line to disconnect.

"How did you get this number?" The suspicion in Bethany's tone was clear.

"A reporter gave it to me in exchange for my story about that day. I told her, I just wanted to speak with you about your father, and your life on the orchard." Cassie cleared her throat. "When was the last time you were out there?"

"Jocelyn. She will not stop harassing me. I guess I shouldn't be surprised. She wants a good story. It must have been pretty important to you to speak with me if you were willing to talk to her to get my details." Bethany paused. "Why would anything that has to do with me be important to you?"

"I'm just trying to get a feel for what happened to James. It was so shocking to come across him that way, and the police are still investigating the crime. I was wondering if maybe you had seen James recently and you knew what might have been going on in his life at the time. I'm just trying to make sense of it all."

"Yes, we were actually at the orchard the day before James was killed." Bethany clucked her tongue. "Now, the police are all over us because of it. Of course we would never do anything to hurt James! We know what it's like to lose a father, we would never do that to someone else."

"I'm so sorry that you had to experience that. Were you and your father close?" Cassie hoped steering the conversation in a new direction would help her feel calmer and more willing to talk.

"We were when I was young. But something changed in him. I don't know if it was the pressure of running the orchard, or maybe he just had regrets, but he became bitter. He was always trying to tug the two of us into the business, but neither of us were interested." Bethany sighed, then paused. When she spoke again, her voice sounded heavy. "I honestly regret selling the orchard. I know it would have broken his heart. But it's what we decided to do. We didn't want it to just fall apart though, or get abandoned, so we made a conditional sale. It allowed us to sell the property quickly and we could continue to be partial owners of the property for ten years from the date of purchase. We were also supposed to get a portion of the profits. It was supposed to be a win-win for us. We'd get the payments for the property over ten years, plus an additional financial boost from the sales."

"But it didn't work out that way?"

"No, James was selling his produce for so cheap that he didn't make a profit, which meant we got nothing from him. We had a meeting with him at the diner shortly after we realized he wasn't paying us anything from the profits of the orchard. He just yelled at us, said there were no profits, business is business. He could price the produce for whatever he wanted. Then a couple of weeks later, we began to hear from other orchards and farms in the area, complaining about his pricing practices." Bethany sighed. "You have to understand, Noah and I know nothing of the business. After our mother died, we really wanted nothing at all to do with home, or the orchard, and I guess in a way, Dad. We didn't realize the damage James was doing to the community until we heard from Zach."

"Do you know Zach well?" Cassie considered how long the two orchard owners might have been neighbors.

"Only in passing. My dad knew him a little better, but they weren't exactly friends. Still, his tip about what was happening at the orchard, is what brought us out there to speak directly with James again. Not just about us, but about what he was doing to the community. He had been avoiding our calls. Noah said we should go, I said we shouldn't, and we both ended up there unprepared for the confrontation. Even though he had argued with us in the diner, his reaction at the orchard was far worse." Bethany drew a sharp breath. "That man wasn't easy to talk to."

"You didn't come to any resolution then?" Cassie jotted a few words down in her notebook.

"Not even close. But I guess none of that matters now. What did you say your name was again?"

"Cassie. Thanks for talking to me, Bethany. I hope that things get resolved for you soon. I'm very sorry for the loss of your father." Cassie paused, hoping that Bethany would fill in a little more information.

"Me too. Maybe if we'd had more time, we could have found our way back to each other." Bethany cleared her throat. "I should go. I probably shouldn't have even spoken to you about any of this. Noah will be upset." She hung up quickly.

Cassie stared at her phone for a moment, then set it down. She would have liked to say more, to try to reassure Bethany, but she doubted that she would welcome a second phone call. As she reviewed the notes she had written, her phone buzzed with a text from Sebastian.

Can't make it today.

Cassie raised an eyebrow as she expected a bit more explanation. Not that he owed it to her, but Sebastian always explained things. The message came off a bit curt, and she wondered if he might be upset with her. She had planned to have the morning free, but without Sebastian to paint with, she wondered what would be the point.

Cassie spent a little time tidying up the house and plotting out how she would fit everyone around her small table for Thanksgiving. Then she stopped at the store to pick up a few of the necessities. Yes, it was possible that no one would show up for dinner, but she planned to make it just the same. As she waited in line to check out, she noticed a man not far behind her. When she looked in his direction, he ducked down the next aisle. She only caught a glimpse of him, but from what she saw, she thought for sure it was Colin. Had he been watching her?

It's the only grocery store in town, Cassie, don't be paranoid. Cassie frowned as she handed over her payment to the cashier. Yes, it was the only grocery store in town, but it sure seemed to her that Colin didn't want to be seen. His presence left an uneasy feeling in the pit of her stomach. Even though she felt uneasy, she wanted to talk to him, but when she went down the aisles to look for him, she couldn't find him. It was like he had vanished.

On Cassie's way out of the grocery store, a missing person poster on the bulletin board by the door caught her attention. It was new, but it was for someone who had gone missing years ago. Mason Johnston. He looked about twenty in the photo.

For some reason she couldn't look away. She shook her head and tried to dismiss the eerie feeling that plagued her. Maybe Oliver's warning had gotten under her skin, and now her nerves were on edge.

CHAPTER 21

After dropping off her groceries, Cassie decided she couldn't just sit around at home waiting for her shift to start. She also couldn't spend it stepping harder on Oliver's toes. If she couldn't go around asking questions about James' murder, she could at least go to work and see if she heard anything that might be helpful. She slipped through the door of the diner and snatched her apron off of the hook before Mirabel could spot her. As she pulled it over her head, she heard the cluck of a tongue and an exasperated sigh.

"You were supposed to be coming in late, remember?" Mirabel put her hands on her hips.

"I know, I know. But I missed you." Cassie smiled sweetly at Mirabel. "Unless you replaced me with someone else. I want to work." She smiled wider. "Besides, Sebastian is taking the day off. So, I might as well work. I'd much rather be here. Working on the house with Sebastian is wearing me out." Her lips twitched around the lie.

"Please." Mirabel rolled her eyes. "You'd much rather be working with Sebastian than me! What are you really up to?"

"Okay, I didn't want to sit at home alone." Cassie tied her apron behind her back.

"Since you're here, you can get to work." Mirabel pointed to a table near the back of the restaurant.

Cassie walked over to the table with a warm smile for the two men seated there. Before she could even speak, one of the men spoke up.

"You're her, aren't you?"

"Excuse me?" Cassie looked into his eyes as her heart skipped a beat. The tension in his expression, mixed in with a bit of sorrow was evident.

"The one who found James?" He shook his head. "Sorry, I didn't expect to see you here, working."

"Oh." Cassie looked between the two men. She couldn't recall having met either of them before. "Did you know James?"

"We worked for him." The second man spoke up. "I'm Alex and this is Grant." He gestured to the other man. "We weren't there the night he died, though. We'd already left for the day."

"I see." Cassie nodded. "I'm very sorry for your loss. Yes, I did find him."

"I'm sorry for that." Alex sighed as he sat back in his chair. "Ever since I heard that it was you, I felt so terrible about it. It must have been horrible to find him that way."

Cassie noted the thickness of his voice. Was he really sorry that the man had died? Was it guilt that brought his emotions to the surface? Did he feel responsible for her finding James' body because he had something to do with James' death?

"Thank you for your concern." Cassie frowned. "It wasn't easy. I just hope that whoever did this will face justice for it."

"Absolutely, justice." Grant nodded.

"Let me get some water for you both." As Cassie walked off she couldn't shake the feeling that the two men were watching her. She knew that as a still fairly new resident of Little Leaf Creek she had the attention of many of the locals, but was it more than that for these two? Were they interested because they thought she might have seen something that would incriminate them? She needed to find out more about where they were the night that James was killed. She walked back over to the table with two glasses of water.

"I honestly can't stop thinking about that day." Cassie paused beside the table. "I wasn't even supposed to be there. I'd gone to Zach's stand to buy some apples, but he wasn't there. I think about where I could have been instead. What if I had just gone home?"

"What if I had stayed to help with the fence?" Grant shook his head. "I think about that all of the time. I promised my wife I'd meet her for dinner, and I wouldn't be late for once. I made sure I left on time. But if I had just stayed, well, maybe I could have helped."

"And done what?" Alex scoffed. "Gotten yourself killed, too?"

"I don't know." Grant shrugged. "I could have done something."

"You were where you were supposed to be. I was where I was supposed to be, too." Alex folded his arms on top of the table as he sat forward. "I went straight to the bar after work, so I could see the game. I'm glad I wasn't there when it all went down. It's not something you get over easy. Is it?"

"No." Cassie shook her head. "Not at all." As she processed their alibis, she realized they were easy enough to verify, and knowing Oliver, he had likely already done that. But she would see if she could find out anything more about them.

After delivering their order to the kitchen, Cassie returned with a pitcher of water to fill their glasses. As she paused beside the table, she felt the pressure of both pairs of eyes on her.

"So, what was it like working with James?" Cassie refilled Grant's drink, which he snatched up right away.

"He was just a cold guy, you know?" Alex shrugged. "Ben could be downright demanding, but he at least made you feel like you had a job worth fighting for. James, he made it clear that we all had an expiration date."

"Even Colin?" Cassie filled Alex's glass.

"Especially Colin! Colin was incredibly loyal to Ben, they had worked together for years." Alex took a sip of water, then set it down. "If Colin hadn't worked hand in hand with Ben and his father for so long, I'm sure James would have fired him the first chance he got. But he knew all of Ben's tricks to keep the orchard thriving, and he would only give James a hint here and there. He knew how to keep his job safe."

"I'm surprised there was so much tension

between the two if Colin knew so much about the orchard. Why do you think they had so many problems?" Cassie set the pitcher of water down on the table and after a quick glance at the other diners, sat down in the empty chair between the two men.

"He and Colin were always going at it, but it got really bad after Colin started stirring things up with the historical society. That was when James and Jackson started really arguing as well."

"Jackson why?" Cassie leaned forward slightly.

"They were getting into it because Jackson didn't want James to get rid of the front porch." Alex rolled his eyes. "Jackson was furious about the idea of James tearing it down."

"Why was Jackson so angry?" Cassie tried to keep her expression neutral. She remembered that Jackson was the youngest of the three men that had been at the farm the day she had found James' body.

"Jackson built the porch with Ben. He was so proud of it. He didn't want it to be torn apart." Alex shook his head. "They worked so hard on the porch."

"Was it just the two of them that worked on it?" Cassie asked.

"Yes, as far as I know." Alex smiled. "I think he had some kind of attachment to Ben, too. Jackson was barely out of school then. I think maybe Ben was taking him under his wing, like a son. They worked on the project together. With Ben gone now, maybe Jackson has a sentimental attachment to the porch."

"The two spent a lot of time together after they built the porch." Grant nodded. "In fact, Jackson was the only one of the workers that Ben would relax and have a drink with."

"So, they were more than employee and boss?" Cassie looked into the man's eyes. "They were friends?"

"I'd say the two were friendlier than Ben and his own son were." Grant spoke up, then frowned. "Not that Ben had any reason to be friendly with his son, or his daughter. The pair of them acted like running the orchard was beneath them, like their father was some kind of embarrassment. They ran off to the city as soon as they could, and whenever they would visit, neither wanted anything to do with the orchard. Ben would try to bring them out to the trees to show them how they were faring, but they both refused and insisted on staying out of the orchard." He winced. "If I had kids like that, I'd want to find someone to replace them, too."

"Easy Grant." Alex swung his foot under the table

and landed a blow against Grant's shin. "Best not to stir up more trouble."

"Oh, you don't have to worry about me stirring up trouble." Cassie waved her hand as she smiled. No, she wasn't stirring up trouble, she was trying to get the truth to surface. If Ben had really taken Jackson under his wing the way these two men claimed, then perhaps Jackson had a motive to go after James. There was of course Colin as well. He might have been following her in the grocery store. Colin and Ben had known each other for years, and Colin appeared to have some loyalty to Ben and wanted to protect the house. Maybe watching James make plans to remodel the house, undercut his deal with Ben's children, and outsell all of the neighboring orchards was enough to make Colin snap. There was only one way to find out.

"Any of that pie left?" Cassie poked her head through the door as she smiled at Tessa.

"Get in here." Tessa laughed. "You've got Harry all worked up."

"Sorry, pal." Cassie crouched down to scratch behind the dog's ears, and allow him a few licks of her cheeks.

"I'll get some pie out for us." Tessa busied herself with the preparations, as Cassie settled in a chair at the table. "I was wondering when you would make your way over here."

"Things have been a little crazy." Cassie shook her head. "Ollie doesn't want me asking too many questions about the murder, and I think I've pushed him a little too far."

"Oh, don't worry about Ollie." Tessa set a piece of pie down in front of Cassie. "He's determined to save the world, whether the world wants saving or not." She sat down across from her with her own piece of pie. "Not that I can blame him, with all of the loss that he's suffered."

"Loss?" Cassie met her eyes.

"It's a long story." Tessa pointed to Cassie's notebook. "Do you have any updates for me?"

Cassie filled her in on her conversation with Bethany, as well as the other information she'd gathered.

"So, your focus is on Colin?" Tessa raised an eyebrow.

"I'm not sure, yet. I know that Ollie is focused on Zach and Kent, at least I think he is, and certainly if Noah and Bethany spoke to James around the time he was killed, they can't be ruled out. But I spotted Colin in the grocery store today when I was picking up some Thanksgiving supplies, and I don't know, it almost felt like he was following me." Cassie frowned. "That sounds a little crazy, doesn't it?"

"Not crazy, no." Tessa narrowed her eyes. "Buying Thanksgiving supplies does sound a little crazy, though."

"Funny." Cassie scrunched up her nose. "I really

do think I should talk to Colin. If he and James had some conflict, as the other workers described, we need to find out about it. And he did organize the petition and the complaint against the renovations."

"I think you're right." Tessa collected their empty plates and set them in the sink. "But if you're going to talk to him, I'm going with you."

"But Ollie—"

"I know all about Ollie trying to boss you around. I'm going to make sure that he doesn't try that again. If he shows up and gives us a hard time, I'll set him straight." Tessa led Cassie out onto the front porch.

"I don't know about that." Cassie frowned as she glanced toward her house. "Ollie doesn't seem like someone who gets set straight too easy."

"You'd better let Sebastian know you can't paint today. If you keep breaking dates with him, he's going to get his feelings hurt."

"They're not dates, we're just fixing up the house." Cassie's cheeks flushed. "And he isn't available today."

"Fixing up the house together, many times a week. Seems to me that Sebastian wants to be more than your handyman."

Cassie bit into her bottom lip as she recalled the invitation to the concert.

"Wait, am I right?" Tessa peered at Cassie. "Did he ask you out on a real date?"

"I don't know what I'm going to do about it, Tessa." Cassie frowned.

"Go out with him, of course." Tessa led the way to Cassie's car. "Why would you do anything else?"

"Why?" Cassie settled in the driver's seat. "I'm a widow to start with, and I haven't been one for that long."

"A widow, true, which is tragic. But my guess is you were alone for quite some time before your husband passed." Tessa raised her eyebrows. "Am I wrong?"

"I don't know how to answer that." Cassie frowned as she started the car.

"Sure you do, you just don't want to be impolite." Tessa sighed as she buckled her seat belt. "One thing I've learned over all of these years, Cassie, is that being polite is an almost complete waste of time. Say what you mean, while you still can." She looked over at her as the car rolled out of the driveway. "It's okay to be honest."

"Honestly, we hadn't been close in a long time. But that didn't make losing him any easier. He was still a huge part of my world, and my life changed completely when I lost him. It feels wrong to be interested in someone new, even though I feel like I've been alone for so long. Besides, Sebastian isn't exactly a safe choice for romance. He's the talk of the town, and who knows if he just wants to have his fun and move on." Cassie shook her head.

"He's not asking you to marry him, Cassie. It's just a date." Tessa laughed. "Give the poor guy a chance, give yourself a chance, what harm could it really do?"

"And have you taken your own advice?" Cassie glanced over at her with a knowing smile. "You should give yourself a chance."

"This isn't about me, this is about you." Tessa looked out through the window. "Do you really think Colin will be out at the orchard? Is it even still operating?"

"That's a quick change of subject." Cassie grinned. "I overheard a few customers talking about the orchard still operating today, so I'm guessing that he'll be there. It's at least a good place to start."

"Someone's here." Tessa tipped her head toward a truck parked near the house.

Cassie nodded as she parked. She stepped out of the car just as Jackson walked up to his truck. She had expected Colin to be there, but she certainly could use the opportunity to ask Jackson some questions.

"The store's closed." Jackson barely glanced at them as he grabbed a shovel from the back of his truck.

"Actually, we're here to talk to you." Cassie walked toward him with Tessa a step behind her.

"Oh, it's you." Jackson stared at her for a moment, then walked toward the orchard. "I can't talk now, I've got a lot of work to do. A few of the guys didn't bother showing up."

"Wait Jackson." Tessa quickened her step. "We just need a few minutes, that's all."

"I said, I don't have a few minutes." Jackson turned to face her.

"We just want to know what's going on with the porch." Cassie's heart pounded as she wondered if the direct approach was the right way to go. "It's so beautiful, and I've heard rumors that it might be destroyed, after you worked so hard on it."

"It's just a porch." Jackson shrugged, and avoided looking in the direction of the porch.

"But you and Colin fought so hard to prevent James from tearing it down. Doesn't it have sentimental value to you?" Cassie peered at him.

"It's just a porch, Cassie. We just wanted to give

James a hard time." Jackson looked straight into her eyes. "It's just a porch on a house I'll never own, part of a property that I will never own. It's nothing to me. Nothing to any of the guys that work here. All that matters is our paychecks, and Bethany has promised me one if I help keep the orchard running until they figure their whole mess out." He walked off and waved his hand at them both. "So stop bothering me."

"Jackson." Cassie started to go after him.

"Don't." Tessa pulled her back. "He's not going to tell us anything else."

"What a waste of time." Cassie sighed.

"Not a total waste." Tessa stared after Jackson. "We know that he's lying. Either he lied about caring about the porch in the first place, or he's lying about it now. That's something."

CHAPTER 23

On the drive back to their houses, Cassie noticed that Tessa remained quiet. As they neared their street, Little Leaf Way, she glanced over at her.

"So, what do you think? What do your instincts tell you?"

"About Jackson?" Tessa continued to stare out the window.

"Yes, about Jackson."

"He's a slippery fellow. Did you notice the way he wouldn't even look at the porch?" Tessa shook her head. "He's up to something. I just can't figure out what."

"Do you think he could have killed James?" Cassie turned down their street.

"I think it's possible. I have no reason to believe that he didn't. He was there, he had the motive of wanting to prevent the porch from being destroyed. Although, that seems like a flimsy motive to me. But his change of attitude toward the porch throws a wrench in his motive. He didn't seem to care about it."

"Maybe that's why he changed his attitude." Cassie slowed down as she neared their houses. "What is Sebastian's truck doing here?"

"Looks like he wasn't too busy for you today after all." Tessa smiled as she stepped out of the car. "Good luck. Remember what I said. Don't overthink it." She tapped the side of her head.

Cassie winced as she nodded. Already, her mind was in overdrive. Had she missed a text from him? Had she stood him up again?

Cassie parked the car, then stepped up onto the porch.

"Hey there." Sebastian glanced over at her as he smiled.

"Hey." Cassie leaned against the post on the porch and stared at him for a moment as guilt washed over her. "I thought you said you couldn't paint today?"

"My plans fell through." Sebastian turned his

attention back to the wall as he ran the roller across it. "I just figured I had nothing better to do, so I might as well get some work done here."

"I'm sure you have a million things that are more important to do." Cassie sighed as she set her purse down on the rocking chair and picked up a paintbrush. "You have an entire farm to run!"

"Eh, this time of year it practically runs itself." Sebastian shrugged as he swept the roller along the wall again.

"How come I don't believe you?" Cassie stepped up beside him and began to paint along the edge of the door. Sebastian never seemed to sleep. He spent long hours working on his farm and still found time to help her out. He seemed to manage to take everything in his stride.

"Would it make you feel better if I said, there's nowhere I'd rather be?" Sebastian lowered the roller as he turned to face her. "Or would that just send you scampering off for the hills?"

Cassie's heart pounded as he looked into her eyes.

As usual, Cassie's mind stirred up all kinds of excuses for his words. He didn't really mean it. He said things like that to all of the girls. He just wanted to see what her reaction would be. But she couldn't look away from him. She couldn't dismiss the warmth and determination that filled those brown eyes, that continued to pin her into place.

"Scampering?" She cleared her throat. "I don't think I've ever scampered in my life."

"No?" Sebastian set the roller down, then looked back at her. "Not even when Tessa's goats get after you?"

"Maybe then." Cassie held her breath as his fingertips, speckled with bits of paint, brushed along her cheek.

"Not now?" Sebastian's voice softened as his touch lingered on the slope of her neck.

Cassie became distinctly aware of just how close he was, with just inches between them, she had to fight two urges. One, to step back, to create a safe distance. The other, and admittedly stronger urge, was to cup his cheeks and press her lips to his. How long had it been since she had experienced a truly wanted kiss? A kiss that just the thought of had her stomach do a flip-flop?

Cassie closed her eyes.

Sebastian's hand settled on her shoulder, and she heard his breath pass slowly across his lips just before he took a step back.

Cassie's eyes fluttered open in time to see him

pick up the roller again. He whistled to himself as he began to run the roller across the wall again.

A mixture of anger and relief left Cassie even more confused as she stared at him.

"I didn't run."

"There's more than one way to run." Sebastian cast a brief smile in her direction. "Lots of work to do." He tipped his head toward the paintbrush in her hand, which steadily dripped paint onto her shoe.

"Oops!" Cassie gave a short laugh, which she hoped broke the tension. He wasn't wrong. She had run. She had been frightened by his advances. But that did nothing to mute the curiosity that he'd set loose within her. If she didn't have a murder to distract her, she might have found herself in a very different moment. Instead, she swept the paintbrush along the wall and tried to focus on the matter at hand.

"I discovered some interesting things today." Cassie began to fill him in on her conversation with the orchard workers. "Did Ben ever talk to you about working on the porch?"

"I tried to discuss it with him one night." Sebastian frowned as he added paint to the roller. "I asked him why he spent so much time on it, when he could have just slapped it together. They'd done such a perfect job, it kind of surprised me that they didn't cut any corners."

"And?" Cassie dipped her paintbrush into the can of paint.

"And he brushed me off. Said he didn't want to talk about it, and to stop asking him about it. I knew he'd been drinking, I just figured that he had a little too much." Sebastian wiped a hand across his face, then frowned. "I guess I should have paid a little more attention."

"You offered your support when Colin filed a complaint against the remodel?" Cassie focused on the motion of her paintbrush, determined not to let her thoughts wander back to the position she'd been in not long before.

"Sure. I agreed with him. The remodel was a violation, and I suspected that Colin felt that he owed it to Ben to try and ensure the house wasn't changed and the porch wasn't destroyed because Ben spent so much time building it. I imagine Jackson felt the same way. I'm sure the porch held some sentimental value to them. I mean, Ben hasn't been gone for that long." Sebastian set the roller down in the pan and grabbed a bottle of water from the porch railing. "As you know, I wasn't a big fan of James either."

"I know." Cassie raised her eyebrows as she glanced at him. "You must have really not liked him. You seem to be a fan of everyone."

"Do I?" Sebastian turned to face her and took another sip of his water. "I do try to keep an open mind about most things. I think getting stuck is one of the worst ways to live. But the way James treated Ben's kids, that was hard for me to overlook. I'd gone out to his orchard to offer him some help with some old machinery he'd intended to sell if he could get it working. I thought maybe I could help him out and try and get him to see reason about undercutting his opposition so badly. But when I arrived, Ben's kids were there, and James shouted at them to get off of his property. The boy, Noah, shouted back that he wasn't going anywhere, that it was still his father's property. James told him he'd run him off if he had to, right along with his sister." His jaw clenched for a long moment, then he shook his head. "I couldn't stand for that. I stepped in and the argument ended real fast. But as Noah was leaving, he shouted at James that he would make sure James honored their deal, by any means necessary." He capped his water bottle and sighed.

"You haven't told Ollie about it?" Cassie looked into his eyes.

"Noah's just a boy, Cassie. If I told Ollie what I heard, I'm sure it would make Noah look pretty suspicious. I just decided to keep quiet about it." Sebastian set the bottle down on the railing again.

"And what if he is guilty?" Cassie watched as he looked out over the road instead of at her. "What if he's the one that killed James, Sebastian?"

"Well then, I've made a terrible mistake, haven't I?" Sebastian picked the roller back up. "But I would never believe he could do that."

assie watched Sebastian work for a few more minutes. Despite the fact that she didn't agree with his decision to withhold information, she couldn't shake the way he spoke of Noah, as if he was his to protect. She'd never met anyone quite like Sebastian before, with such a huge heart, and so much determination to be loyal to everyone around him. Maybe the problem was, he didn't have that same feeling toward James.

"This must be so hard for you."

Sebastian set the roller down again and turned to look at her. "We're losing light. I guess we'd better be done for the night."

"Okay." Cassie stepped up beside him. "I'm sorry, Sebastian."

"For?" Sebastian looked into her eyes.

"I've been treating this like a mystery, like something I need to solve. I've been talking about your friends, the people of this town, as if they're potential suspects. But they're so much more than that to you, aren't they?" Cassie wiped a drop of paint from his cheek. "They're your friends, maybe even your family."

"When you've lived in the same town, with the same people for so long, they become like family." Sebastian caught her hand as it fell away from his cheek. "But you don't have to apologize. Yes, I care about the people in this town. But if one of them committed murder, I absolutely want to know who did it, and I want them to pay for it." He held her gaze. "If I had thought Noah was capable of this, I would have said something to Ollie."

"Just like Zach?" Cassie murmured her words as his rich brown eyes continued to search hers.

"He's a good man."

"An angry man." Cassie felt his fingers curl tighter around her hand.

"I didn't know he would treat you like that."

"But you knew he could get very drunk and very angry, didn't you?" Cassie drew her hand from his.

"We all have our problems." Sebastian lowered his eyes as his jaw rippled with tension. "Zach's life was falling apart around him."

"Sebastian."

"I have to go." Sebastian started down the porch steps, then paused at the bottom one and looked back up at her. "Maybe you should hire someone to finish this up, Cassie. I'm going to be pretty busy with the late harvest."

Stunned, Cassie couldn't respond as he walked over to his truck. When he warned her about pushing too hard with Tessa, maybe she should have applied that warning to him, too. As she heard his door slam shut, she wondered if it would be the last time.

The truck pulled away. Cassie turned to face her front door, which led to nothing but too much space. Instead of going in, she headed over to Tessa's house.

"He pulled out of here fast, didn't he?" Tessa watched the pickup truck disappear down the road from her perch on the front porch.

"I don't want to talk about it." Cassie sighed. "Can we talk about Noah and Bethany, instead?" She patted Harry on the head.

"Sure, come inside." Tessa pushed open the front door.

"They really stand to benefit the most financially from this situation, I think." Cassie followed her into the kitchen with Harry close behind.

"So, you think there might be some motive there?" Tessa pulled out a chair for her, then sat down in the one she preferred.

"I think there might be, yes." Cassie settled in the chair. "I was under the impression that the orchard would pass on to James' wife and children, but now I wonder if there might have been some stipulation in their deal that stated otherwise. I don't know for sure, but maybe they get the property back?"

"Interesting thought. I do know the deal they struck was a bit unconventional. Luckily, I have a source that might be able to give us some insight into it." Tessa stood up and grabbed her phone off the counter. "I'll see if I can get us an appointment to see him."

"Who is it?" Cassie reached down to pet Harry who nuzzled her knee.

"Mark Collingswood, he's a lawyer. If anyone needs anything legal done around here, they usually go to him. He's a bit of a jack-of-all-trades when it comes to the law. I would have called him when you were suspected of murder, but he was on vacation at the time." Tessa put the phone to her ear, paused a moment, then spoke again. "Hi Elizabeth, I'd like to make an appointment with Mark if that's alright. Yes, just tell him it's for Tessa." She paused again, then smiled. "I appreciate him making room in his schedule for me. Is he free now?" She looked over at Cassie and nodded. "Great, I'll be right over." She ended the call.

"We'll be right over?" Cassie stood up. "I hope?"

"Sure." Tessa smiled as she tossed a treat to Harry. "I wouldn't want you to miss out on meeting Mark. He's quite a spectacle."

Intrigued, Cassie followed her out the door.

As Tessa drove through the streets of Little Leaf Creek, Cassie began to recognize the things around her. The small town had really become a new home to her. Although, not everyone accepted her, she had already begun to accept all of them. Her thoughts wandered to Oliver and the tension between them.

"Here we are." Tessa pulled up to a two-story office building with several doors facing the parking lot and an open air stairway leading up to the second floor. "He's up top in the corner." She stepped out of her jeep, then waited for Cassie to join her.

Cassie stepped out and peered up at the window

that overlooked the parking lot. She saw some movement in it, then the door swung open, and a man walked up to the second floor railing.

"Tessa! Get up here, you stunning specimen of a woman!"

Tessa rolled her eyes. "Settle down, Mark, it's an appointment, not a date."

Cassie's eyes widened as Mark's laughter boomed across the parking lot. It seemed to her that the man didn't have any sense of volume control.

"Don't worry," Tessa muttered to Cassie as she led the way up the stairs. "He's all bark."

"Oh, come here, Tessa. It's good to see you." Mark winked at Tessa as he pulled her into a warm hug.

Stunned, Cassie watched as Tessa tolerated the embrace. Never once had she considered Tessa to be someone who welcomed hugs. Maybe there was another side to her that she hadn't seen, or she was willing to tolerate the embrace for the sake of the investigation.

"Enough, enough." Tessa shook him loose and took a step back. "This is my friend."

"Cassie!" Mark grinned. "I've been waiting for a chance to meet you. You're the talk of the town."

"Oh, I'm not very interesting I'm afraid." Cassie

took a slight step back, just in case he decided to hug her as well. Mark appeared to be in his sixties, maybe a bit younger. His stark white hair still flowed thick from the top of his head, and his bright green eyes peered out at them from behind rectangular glasses. What he lacked in physical size, he made up for in the brightness of his suit. Lime green, combined with a bright pink tie. Cassie was sure if she blinked he might turn out to be a figment of her imagination.

"Come inside, I've got drinks for us." Mark held open the door for both women.

The office was just about as loud as Mark's suit, with red leather and metal studs scattered throughout the decor.

"Elizabeth dear, bring our drinks into my office, and hold my calls." Mark led the way into a smaller space, separated by two walls of glass.

Elizabeth, a young woman dressed in a conservative, dark blue pants suit with straight, black hair, gathered some glasses from a bar in the corner.

"Sit, sit." Mark gestured to two chairs that looked more like bar stools in front of his desk.

"Thanks." Cassie wriggled onto one of the stools.

Tessa rolled her eyes and grabbed a wooden chair near one of the walls. She pulled it over beside Cassie.

"We're here on business, Mark."

"Business?" Mark settled in his large, leather chair as Elizabeth delivered their drinks. "What kind of business? You're not in some kind of trouble, are you?"

"No, not in any trouble." Tessa smiled at Elizabeth as she took her glass. "Thanks Elizabeth." She turned her attention back to Mark. "I need some information from you, and before you start trying to wheel and deal, let's be clear, you owe me."

"Tessa, I would never charge you a dime." Mark looked straight into her eyes, then sighed. "So, what information do you need?"

"I need to know about the deal you struck for James Rallow to buy the orchard." Tessa stared straight into his eyes. "With James dead, who owns it now?"

"Now, now, not so fast. That's private information." Mark quirked an eyebrow, then laughed. "But what's private between friends, right? Just keep it between these four walls." He winked at them both. "The sale was not complete. It wouldn't have been complete until he had made payments for ten years. Then he would be the full owner of the property. Since he had not reached that point, the property ownership reverts to Bethany and Noah."

"Thank you." Tessa stood up.

Cassie stood up as well.

"Wait just a second, don't you want to know the best part?" Mark's eyes seemed to shine as they locked onto Tessa.

"What's that?" Tessa paused near the door of the office and looked back at him.

Cassie watched the tension crackle between the two, though she sensed a hint of amusement from Mark as well.

"Noah called me, the day that James died. He wanted to make sure that the deal was ironclad, that there was no way it could be disputed." Mark lowered his voice. "He asked me if James' wife would have any claim to the property if something were to happen to James. He wanted to know if she continued to pay for the property would it stay in her name."

"What?" Cassie gasped. "Have you told Oliver this?"

"The detective?" Mark gave a short laugh. "Not a

chance. I couldn't betray my client like that. Don't you bother telling him what I said either, I will deny it." He looked back over at Tessa. "But keep in mind, I told you the truth."

"Yes, you did." Tessa gazed at him for a long moment, then pushed open the door.

s Cassie and Tessa settled back into the jeep, Cassie could barely catch her breath.

"That's it! Bethany and Noah did it! Right, Tessa?" She turned toward Tessa.

"It sure seems that way." Tessa started the car.

"So, why aren't you more excited?" Cassie frowned.

"Because it's just strange, don't you think? If you were planning to kill someone, to get them out of your way, would you risk calling your lawyer and asking such specific questions? Would you then just walk up to the man, out of the blue, and kill him? He could have waited until James was in his car, or sleeping, or off on a trip. He could have done it at any time. So, why did he do it when other employees were there and customers might stop by his shop?" Tessa headed in the direction of home.

"That's true, but all of the farmhands were off doing projects around the orchard. Maybe he knew that somehow. Maybe he had spoken to one of them." Cassie's mind was spinning with the possibilities. "We have to tell Ollie."

"We can tell him, but without Mark backing our information up, I'm not sure it will lead to much." Tessa frowned as she pulled up in front of her house. "Are you coming in?"

"I want to go see if I can speak to Ollie again. Maybe he has something else to offer." Cassie got out of the jeep. "I can at least mention Bethany and Noah."

"I'll make a few calls as well. Maybe I can confirm what Noah was up to that day. If so, then we might have some more substantial information to give to Ollie."

"Okay, great idea." Cassie walked toward her car.

"Okay. I'll catch up with you later." Tessa turned toward her house.

Cassie was on the way to the police station mulling over what she knew so far about the case, when she changed her mind. She headed toward the highway instead, deciding that she wanted to speak to Bethany in person. She was sure she would be able to get more information out of her that way.

Cassie would have rather spoken to Noah, but she didn't know where he lived, and after a quick search couldn't find his address. She hoped that Bethany would reveal what she knew about her brother's intentions concerning the orchard.

As Cassie walked up to the front door of Bethany's house, she realized that Bethany wasn't alone inside. She could hear her voice, and a very distinct male voice. They both sounded very angry. She paused in front of the door and listened.

"You shouldn't be doing this! Every time you argue with that detective, he gets more ammunition against us!" The male voice shouted. "It makes us look even more guilty! You have to think about what you're doing right now, every single second. Bethany, I told you just tell him what he wants to hear!"

"Me?" Bethany shouted back. "That's rich coming from you, Noah! You, who lost your temper with James for anyone to hear! Talk about making us look guilty! What were you thinking?"

"Keep quiet, Bethany!" Noah snarled his words.

Through the front window, Cassie caught sight of Noah shouting at his sister. He towered over her, pointing his finger at her. He looked very angry and intimidating.

Cassie held in a gasp and took a step back from the door.

"You don't know what you're talking about! James pushed me too far! I had no choice!"

Cassie's heart raced as she wondered if the words she'd just heard were a confession. Though she was tempted to confront the siblings, she thought the better option to catch them, was to call Oliver so he could arrest them.

Cassie pulled out her phone and dialed Oliver's number. He picked up on the third ring.

"Cassie? Is everything okay?"

"I don't think so, Ollie. I'm at Bethany's house, she's here with her brother Noah. I've been listening to them fight, and I'm pretty sure they're arguing about killing James!"

"What?" Oliver's voice sharpened. "Where are you right now? Are you still there?"

"Yes, I'm right outside the door." Cassie held her breath as she realized that she no longer heard the voices from inside. "Noah's so angry, Ollie, I'm afraid he might do something to hurt Bethany."

"I'll be right there. But you need to get somewhere safe. Understand?"

"Sure, I do." Cassie swallowed hard as she ended the call.

She started to turn away from the house, to head back to her car, but before she could, the front door swung open.

"What are you doing out here?" Noah glared at her, then looked over his shoulder at his sister. "Do you know this woman?"

"Who are you?" Bethany stared at her.

"We spoke on the phone, Bethany, I'm Cassie." She tried to disguise the tremble in her hand as she held it out to Noah. "I'm just here to help."

"To help?" Noah ignored her hand, then looked past her at her car. "Are you alone?"

"Yes, I'm alone." Cassie answered without thinking. A second later, her cheeks flushed. "I mean, other people know that I'm here."

"What kind of answer is that?" Bethany frowned.

"An answer that tells us she just heard everything we said." Noah grabbed Cassie by the arm. "You need to come inside."

"Wait, please!" Cassie tried to pull free of his grip. "I didn't hear anything at all. I just came up, and I did hear some commotion, like you two might be fighting, so I thought it might not be a good time for a visit. I was just going to go back to my car. I don't know what you're arguing about, but whatever it is, I'm sure you can work it out. You're brother and sister after all."

"Are we?" Noah glared at her. "How do you know that? Neither of us told you that we're siblings."

"I don't know." Cassie's throat grew dry as she realized her mistake. "I just assumed, I guess. I know that siblings fight sometimes."

"Let's go." Noah tugged her inside the house.

"Noah, what are you doing!" Bethany shrieked at him and grabbed Cassie's other arm. "Let her go! You can't just pull her into the house! That's kidnapping!"

"Am I just supposed to let her run off and tell everyone what she just heard?" Noah glared at his sister. "How do you think that's going to go, when good old Ollie hears about this?"

"I don't know, but that doesn't mean we can do this." Bethany shook her head and let go of Cassie's arm. "This is all out of control now. We have to slow down and think things through."

"Yes." Cassie nodded as she felt Noah's grip loosen on her arm. "That's all you need to do. I'm not going to tell anyone. I don't even know this Ollie—"

"Cassie!" Oliver shouted her name as he jogged up to the still open front door of the house.

"Don't know him, huh?" Noah rolled his eyes and pushed her away from him, and right into Oliver as he stepped through the door. "Well, isn't this just perfect?" He turned to face Bethany. "Now, look what you've done!"

Oliver pulled his shoulders back as he glared at Bethany and Noah.

"Someone needs to tell me what is going on here right now!"

"I'll tell you what's going on." Noah glared at him. "You just barged into my sister's house without a warrant or cause."

"From what I heard, I have every cause." Oliver stepped between Cassie and the siblings. "If you think you're going to put your hands on her again you have lost your mind."

"This is all a big mistake!" Bethany gasped out her words as she covered her face with her hands. "Please Ollie, let me explain!"

"You can explain down at the station." Oliver motioned for her to turn around.

"I'm calling my lawyer." Noah reached for his phone in his pocket.

"Stop right there!" Oliver barked at him, as he put his hand on his gun.

"Stop it!" Bethany shouted. "We didn't kill

anyone! We didn't hurt James! Please don't hurt my brother, he's all I have left!"

"It's just my phone!" Noah held his hands up in the air. "I'm not armed!"

Oliver grabbed Noah by the arm. He patted him down in search of a weapon, then shook his head.

"As I said, everyone needs to calm down. Bethany, sit down there, please." Oliver pointed to a chair not far from him.

"Please." Bethany sobbed as she followed his instructions. "We didn't hurt James."

"But you do get the property back now that James is dead?" Cassie stepped back as Oliver shot a glare in her direction.

"We do." Noah took a step toward her, but froze as Oliver's eyes locked onto him. "But we never wanted the orchard back. All I heard from the workers at the orchard, and the ones who don't work there anymore, is how much they disliked James. I've heard rumors about him and Colin going toe to toe. I also overheard Kent and Zach discussing something at the diner that left me unsettled. So, I checked to find out what would happen if James got himself into so much trouble that he ended up dead. I had hoped the property would go to his wife and she would have to honor the deal and continue to pay us so we wouldn't have to worry about finding another buyer for the orchard and hopefully she would price the fruit fairly, so the deal between us and James was properly honored. And my dad's business would be taken care of. But that's not how we have it set up in our agreement."

"Now, it's a huge mess." Bethany shook her head. "The last thing we want is the orchard. But until we find another buyer, we don't have a choice now. We have to keep it running because those men depend on their paychecks. And it's still our father's business. You should see how much harder they had to work for James for the same or even less pay!"

"If anyone wanted James dead, it would be one of the workers." Noah shook his head. "My father might not have been a great guy, but he did treat his workers fairly."

"Especially Jackson." Bethany nodded. "He paid him more than any of the other workers. I asked him about it once, and he nearly took my head off. Just told me to leave it alone. I never understood why. But he also made me promise him that if anything happened to him, we would continue to pay Jackson the same amount, and to make sure that all of the workers were treated well. Of course we had no control over that once James took over the property."

"We didn't do this." Noah looked straight at Oliver. "You can arrest me if you want to. I know I shouldn't have grabbed Cassie like that. But please, leave my sister out of this. She had nothing to do with any of it. We just wanted to be free of the orchard. It turned our father sour, it made him bitter. We don't want that for ourselves. That's why when James offered us this unusual purchase deal, we went for it. We just wanted to get rid of the orchard as soon as possible. But also try to make sure it was okay."

"I'm not pressing charges." Cassie spoke up as her heart pounded. She realized as she began to fit the pieces of the puzzle together, that Noah and Bethany didn't quite fit. Either they were great actors, or they really didn't want the orchard.

Oliver sighed, then shook his head.

"I don't have any reason to arrest either of you at this point, if Cassie is refusing to press charges. But you're both going to need to come in and fill out a statement. I need details, about everything you mentioned here. I want to know who had a problem with James and why. I want to know what the two of you discussed the last time you saw him. I would like financial records for both of you as well."

"You don't have any right to ask us for those." Noah frowned.

"Enough Noah." Bethany nodded at Oliver. "We'll provide all of it, Ollie. Just please, find James' real killer, before this whole thing ruins our lives."

"That's exactly what I'm trying to do." Oliver shot a brief look at Cassie, then turned and walked out of the house.

As Cassie followed after him, she sensed the tension in every step he took, the tightness of his shoulders, and his refusal to look at her. Without a word he got into his car and pulled away. She stared after him for a moment, then got into her own car. Her heart sank as she realized she might have made a huge mess of things. Thanksgiving wasn't looking like a possibility anymore.

CHAPTER 26

As Cassie started her car with the intention of driving straight to Tessa's, she got a text from Mirabel asking if she could come help out for a bit. She replied that she was on her way. As much as she wanted to talk to Tessa about what she had discovered, she knew that if Mirabel had contacted her she must be really busy. It was unlike Mirabel to ask for help and after being distracted at work recently she was glad that she could help her out.

When Cassie arrived at the diner, her mind was spinning from the events of the afternoon. But she couldn't think about it for long as the diner was packed. She could see why Mirabel needed the help. The afternoon wasn't usually a busy time, but both the book club and knitting club were there, as well as other diners. And Mirabel was working alone.

Cassie waved to the customers she knew as she walked behind the counter to put on her apron.

"You're a lifesaver." Mirabel called out as she rushed toward the kitchen. A few seconds later she came back out. "Thank you so much, Cassie." Mirabel rushed up to her with a tray of food. "Table ten."

"No problem." Cassie plastered on a smile and grabbed the tray.

The diner was packed for the next couple of hours. Cassie and Mirabel were flat out and they barely said two words to each other.

When they finally hit a lull, Cassie stepped up to the sink to start catching up with the dishes. As she washed the dishes, she thought about Thanksgiving and whether she could convince Tessa and Oliver to join her.

After a few minutes Mirabel joined her at the sink.

"Well, that was crazy!" Mirabel smiled as she picked up a bowl. "Thank you again for coming in at such short notice."

"Of course. I'm glad I could help." Cassie nodded.

"Mirabel, you know about everyone around here, right?" She glanced over at her.

"I know more than I'd like about most." Mirabel nodded. "Why?"

"I'm just curious about Oliver's family." Cassie rinsed off a plate and set it out on the rack to dry.

"He doesn't really have any left." Mirabel dropped the bowl she had been washing. It clanged loudly against the bottom of the metal sink.

"Siblings?" Cassie picked up the bowl and checked it over for chips, then rinsed it off.

"No, he's an only child." Mirabel began to wash another bowl.

"What about his parents?" Cassie rinsed the next bowl, then stepped back from the sink.

"Orville and Alice had a terrible divorce." Mirabel turned to face her and looked her square in the eye. "He treated her really badly at a time when she really needed him."

"Alice?" Cassie gasped. "As in Tessa's Alice?"

"Yes." Mirabel nodded. "Didn't you know?"

"No, I didn't realize." Cassie's mouth fell open.

"I'm not really surprised I guess, he doesn't talk about it. Alice passed away when Oliver was young and he went to live with his father at the time. I think they were trying to protect him." Mirabel picked up the towel. "It was very sad."

"So, what happened between Tessa and Oliver that there is so much tension?"

"I don't know the whole story." Mirabel shook her head. "I know they had a disagreement when they worked together on the police force. They were on a job and Tessa landed up getting shot when she was protecting Oliver. Apparently, Oliver was angry with her for not following the rules."

"But there must be more to the story. I just don't understand what the problem is between the two of them that they can't move forward. Why it can't be solved." Cassie nodded. "They need each other."

"There's no question that they do." Mirabel smiled. "But you're not going to fix what's broken between them, only they can do that."

"I know." Cassie shrugged. "But I can try to help. A friendship like that doesn't just disappear."

"Tessa and Alice were very close and Oliver always looked up to Tessa, especially after Alice passed away. He wanted to be a cop just like her." Mirabel nodded. "Personally, I think he's a nice guy. He seems reasonable enough. But he takes everything so seriously." She turned back to the sink.

"He does seem pretty tense." Cassie frowned. "He

never speaks about his family. I mean, I didn't even know Alice was his mother. Is Orville still alive?"

"No, Orville passed away a few years back now. And of course Alice passed away years ago." Mirabel tipped her head toward the door. "Thanks again for coming in, Cassie. Tamera is coming in soon."

"Happy to help." Cassie took off her apron. "See you tomorrow." She waved as she walked out the door.

As Cassie walked toward her car, she thought about what she had just found out about Oliver.

Did Oliver have anyone in his life that he could call family?

Cassie's mind swirled as she drove home. She wanted to speak to both Oliver and Tessa about what she had found out about their connection to Alice and each other, but she didn't want to push them away. She needed to work out the best way to bring up the subject with them, so they didn't close off completely. She wasn't sure if Oliver would even speak to her after the way he reacted earlier.

Cassie decided to leave it alone for the moment and try to get Tessa's advice on James' murder. She still hadn't spoken to her about the mess she had made with Oliver over Bethany and Noah.

CHAPTER 27

Cassie arrived at Tessa's house, her mind fuzzy, and her frustration level high. When she knocked on the door, Tessa opened it with a frown.

"Leaving me out of things again, are you?"

"Making a huge mess, is more like it. Can I come in?"

"There's a bit of pie left." Tessa nodded as she stepped away from the door.

Moments later, they both had a cup of coffee and a slice of pie. Harry gnawed on a bit of crust that Cassie tossed to him.

Cassie blurted out her encounter with Bethany and Noah, as well as Oliver's icy behavior.

"I think he hates me now." She sighed. "And we're no closer to figuring out who did this."

"Actually, we can rule Noah out. I found out from an acquaintance that he was with her son playing something called frisbee golf in the park. I have no idea what that is, but I trust she's telling me the truth." Tessa wiped her hand across her face. "That doesn't rule Bethany out, though."

"I don't know, Tessa. The way they spoke about the orchard, I just don't think they wanted it. They seem to think it changed their father for the worse."

"I remember the change in Ben they're talking about." Tessa dug her fork into the pie, but didn't take a bite. "He was always involved in community events before then. Especially that year in particular. He hired on a few new men to work in the orchard, because his harvest was so good. He was due to participate in the town festival, lead the parade, and participate in a drive for charity. But he didn't. It was a bit of a scandal when he canceled at the last minute. After that, I started to hear people talking about his change in behavior. I never thought too much about it, but now that you mentioned it, it sticks out like a sore thumb to me. Something must have happened during that time to cause such a big change in him." She took a sharp breath, then narrowed her eyes. "Now that I think about it, that was the same year that he built that porch."

"Really?" Cassie met her eyes. "There has to be something about that porch that I'm missing."

"The porch?" Tessa nodded slowly as she looked at her. "I suppose, but it's not as if the porch murdered anyone."

For just an instant, Cassie imagined that Ben himself had come back from the dead to seek revenge on James for wanting to destroy his porch and not treating the workers properly. She dismissed the thought and shook her head.

"No it's not, I know that." Cassie sighed. "And maybe I'm grasping at straws here, but for some reason my mind keeps going back to that porch."

"One of the things I learned in my years as a police officer, is to always trust your instincts. You can't necessarily put all of the weight of a case on them, but following a hunch is always better than following nothing. If you think it has something to do with the porch, then let's focus on that." Tessa knocked her knuckles against the table. "It was a time of change for Ben. Jackson is tight-lipped about building the porch. But he wasn't the only one working on the property when the porch was built."

"I've asked some of the other workers at the

orchard about it, and they don't seem to know much more." Cassie frowned, then met Tessa's eyes. "Wait a minute, didn't you say that he hired some new workers during that time? Because the orchard was doing so well?"

"Yes, he did." Tessa narrowed her eyes. "I don't recall their names, some of them weren't from around here. I think he hired on three or four new guys."

"There should be some kind of record of that, shouldn't there?" Cassie stood up and grabbed her computer. "Maybe if we dig a little deeper we'll be able to find someone that was there during that time, and knows something about what happened while the porch was being built."

"Maybe, I think it's worth a shot." Tessa watched as Cassie began to search through local websites. "But I doubt you'll find anything there. Let me see if one of my contacts can get me the information. She might be able to access the employment records."

Cassie continued to search as Tessa pulled out her phone and went into the other room to make the call.

A few minutes later Tessa walked back in.

"Apparently, he added four new employees that

year. There's only one who doesn't still work there." Tessa sat back down. "Mason Johnston."

"Do you remember him?" Cassie jotted down the name. For some reason it sounded familiar to her.

"No, I can't say I remember him." Tessa shook her head. "Apparently, he only worked there for a few months."

Cassie added the duration to her list.

"All of the other men have stayed on for much longer. I wonder why he was there for such a short time?"

"Maybe he just decided to move on? Sometimes people pass through and pick up work during their travels."

"True." Cassie pursed her lips. "I think I'll have Ollie look into him, though, just out of curiosity. If nothing comes of it, then I guess I've just hit another dead end." She pulled out her phone, then frowned. "Then again he might not be in the mood to hear from me right now." She narrowed her eyes. "Maybe I'll call that reporter Jocelyn, I bet she has some contacts that can help me out."

"Things are that bad with Ollie, huh?" Tessa gazed off into space for a moment, then shook her head.

"I hope not, I hope we can repair our friendship."

Cassie looked up at her as she dialed Jocelyn's number.

Cassie opened her mouth to ask something, but before she could Jocelyn answered.

"Hey there, Cassie, I was hoping to hear from you again."

"Perfect, because I have a favor to ask of you."

"What can I do to help?"

"I need you to look up a name for me. Mason Johnston."

"Mason?" Jocelyn took a sharp breath. "Why?"

"Do you know him?"

"I know of him, yes. He's the reason I came to Little Leaf Creek in the first place. I was investigating his disappearance when James was killed."

Cassie's mind flashed back to the missing person poster in the grocery store. That's where she had seen the name.

"He went missing?"

"Yes. Well, according to his mother he did. She reported him missing from Ben's orchard, but Ben showed the police a letter he had left behind stating that he was quitting and that he would be traveling for a while. Mason's mother never believed it was written by her son, but the police insisted that it was enough evidence to prove that he wasn't missing. Adults are adults, and they can roam as they please. Only, there was something she was too ashamed to tell them. Ben wasn't just Mason's employer, he was his father. She had an affair with Ben. She had confessed this to Mason, and that was the reason he'd gone to find Ben." She sighed. "She came to me with her story a few months ago. I was going to dismiss it, too, until I couldn't find a single trace of Mason anywhere. He never got a parking ticket, never cast a vote, never bought or rented a home. A person doesn't just disappear, not out of the blue like that."

Cassie frowned as she wondered how Mason could be connected to all of this. "Do you think something happened to him?"

"Honestly, I think he's dead. I don't want to tell his mother that, but I do suspect it. I put up some posters around Little Leaf Creek. I had hoped to get some information out of James, but he didn't know anything about the former employees. He directed me to Jackson, one of the employees that still works for the orchard, but he insisted he had no idea about Mason, didn't even remember him. Then James was killed, and I suspected there was a bigger story to chase."

"Do you think James' murder and Mason's disappearance could be connected?" Cassie looked across the table at Tessa, whose eyes widened.

"I'm not sure. I don't see how they could be. I haven't found a single connection between Mason and James. It's tough, I'm at a bit of a dead end. But I'm not ready to give up. Do you have any new information for me?"

"Not much really. Nothing that sticks." Cassie frowned. "Hopefully, we'll turn up something soon."

"Let me know!"

Cassie ended the call and shook her head.

"I don't think Mason could be involved with the murder, and we're certainly not going to get any information out of him about it. Jocelyn suspects that he is dead."

"Dead? How?" Tessa narrowed her eyes.

"She doesn't know. There's been no sign of him. But the odd thing is, Ben had a letter from him saying he was quitting to go travel. But Mason's mother insisted that he would never do that, and my guess is that she would know. Although, I'm sure sons don't always tell their mothers everything." Cassie sat back in her chair and tapped her fingertips against the table. "Apparently, Mason was actually Ben's son. He wasn't really there to work.

How do you think Ben reacted when Mason told him the truth? I wonder if he even had the chance to."

"I wonder." Tessa frowned. "It looks like it's another dead end."

"I think we need to go out to that orchard again. I want to get a look at that place again. Maybe there's something I didn't notice when I found James. Maybe something will bring back a memory I've overlooked." Cassie met Tessa's eyes. "What do you think?"

"I think it's worth a try, and Harry here could use a good walk." Tessa scratched behind his ears. "Maybe he'll sniff us out a clue or two."

"Great idea." Cassie smiled. She tried to get what she now knew about Alice out of her mind so she could focus on finding James' murderer.

CHAPTER 28

It was almost dark as Cassie and Tessa pulled into the driveway of James' orchard. A shiver carried down Cassie's spine as she remembered approaching the shop for apples and finding James' body.

"Are you okay?" Tessa glanced over at her.

"Yes, fine." Cassie stepped out of the car.

Tessa stepped out as well, with Harry right behind her. "It's quiet. I guess everyone has gone home for the night."

"It is a beautiful porch, isn't it?" Cassie gazed at it, drawn to its pillars and railing. It all looked hand carved. "But why did Ben build it in the first place? From everything I've learned about him, he doesn't seem like the type to spend money on frivolous things, and it was a fight to build it, wasn't it?"

"Yes, I suppose it was." Tessa frowned as she held onto Harry's leash. "Settle down, pup!"

Harry gave a sharp bark, then lunged toward the front porch.

"I guess he likes it, too." Cassie smiled. Her phone buzzed again. A quick glance revealed it was from Sebastian. She was tempted to read it, but she knew it would distract her. Instead she turned her phone to silent, determined to focus only on James' murder. She didn't want to be distracted when she spoke to him. Whatever was going on between her and Sebastian would have to wait, even if that meant that he became more annoyed with her. As she recalled the way he'd walked away, her stomach twisted into a knot.

James, she reminded herself. Finding James' murderer was what needed her attention. Cassie glanced back at the spot on the driveway where she'd found him. A subtle crunch drew her attention to the trail beside them that led out to the orchard. She swung the light from the flashlight on her phone down the path. Satisfied that it must have been a squirrel, she turned her attention back to the porch. "I'm going to take a closer look."

"I think Harry wants to, too." Tessa laughed as she let the dog pull her forward.

Cassie started up the steps of the front porch, while Harry led Tessa around the side of it. As she studied the details of the structure, she tried to picture how Ben must have felt as he built it. Did he build it before he found out he had another son? Did he already know about Mason? Was his bond with Jackson an attempt to replace the bond he never had with Mason? She looked at Tessa who struggled to pull Harry out from under the porch.

"Cassie!" Tessa gasped as she stumbled back away from the porch.

"What is it?" Cassie heard the alarm in her friend's voice and ran up beside her just in time to see Harry drag something out from under the porch. The area around the porch had been dug up. Cassie's chest tightened as she stared down at the dirt-covered object. "Tessa, is that a bone?"

"Yes." Tessa crouched down and shooed Harry away from it. She looked up at Cassie with wide eyes. "And it's human."

Cassie's heart pounded as a story began to form in her mind, one that she had a hard time believing, until she felt something shoved into her back.

"Cassie!" Tessa stood up quickly. "Jackson! Let her go!"

Cassie realized that the object in her back was the barrel of a gun.

"I can't do that." Jackson wrapped his free hand around Cassie's arm and held it tight. "If you move a muscle, if you reach for your phone, or if you let that dog loose on me, she's going to die right here and right now."

"I'm not going to do anything, Jackson, please." Tessa's lips trembled as she spoke.

It crossed Cassie's mind that she'd never seen Tessa so afraid before. Tessa's fear made Cassie even more nervous.

"Jackson, this is just a mistake. It's alright. Dogs find bones all of the time." Cassie tried to keep her voice steady, despite the panic that filled her.

"Sure, sure." Jackson chuckled. "Let's all try running that one by dear old Oliver. Don't worry, Ollie, the dog just dug up some old animal bones. Sure, plenty of animals have human skulls."

"Ollie never has to hear about this at all." Cassie shuddered. "Whatever happened here, Jackson, I'm sure that it wasn't your fault."

"It wasn't." Jackson released her arm, then stepped around in front of her so that he could point the gun at both of them. "It wasn't my fault at all. But of course, I'm the one that got stuck in the middle of all of it."

"Tell me what happened." Cassie had no idea whether buying them some time would make any difference, but it was the only option she could think of to keep them alive a little longer. "It was Ben's fault, wasn't it? Because Mason was his son?"

Jackson's eyes widened as he stared at her.

"You know about that?"

"I do." Cassie nodded. "But not as much as you do, I'm sure."

"That was it. Ben offered to pay him some money to stay out of his life. He didn't want to mess things up with his wife and kids. But Mason wanted more than that. He threatened to tell his family all about it, and Ben lost it. He killed Mason, right there, in front of me. Then he told me that I had to help him cover it up." Jackson groaned. "What could I do? I watched him murder a man! I thought I would be next! So, I started digging. We dug a hole right in front of the house, to hide the blood that was on the ground."

"But that wasn't enough, was it?" Cassie met his eyes.

"No. It wasn't. The cops came out to take a look around. Stood right on the grave. Ben nearly lost his mind. He said we had to make sure the body couldn't be found. So, we built a porch over it, to help hide it."

"Which is why you didn't want James tearing it down." Tessa held tight to Harry's leash. "Because you were afraid someone would find Mason's body?"

"Yes, that's why. It was bad enough when James started talking about expanding the house and tearing down the porch. I managed to convince Colin to fight to protect Ben's house. I said it was what Ben would want. He wouldn't want the porch destroyed. But then that reporter came sniffing around." Jackson shook his head as he continued to point the weapon at both of them. "Claimed she was investigating a missing person. Mason. She asked James about him, and James asked me to tell her what I knew about him. Of course, I couldn't do that. I knew that it was all starting to unravel, though. With James wanting to get rid of the porch, and the reporter getting curious about Mason, I knew it was just a matter of time before his body would be discovered."

"So, you had to do something?" Cassie prompted.

"Yes. James was supposed to be working the shop, and Miah and Colin were busy with their projects. Everyone else had gone for the day. It seemed like the right time to get under the porch and just have a look. But James caught me right when I uncovered Mason's skeleton. I had no choice but to kill him. I was going to get rid of his body, too, but I had to cover up Mason's remains first, and by the time I did that, you showed up. I haven't had the opportunity to get rid of it since." Jackson scowled as he looked at Cassie. "And here you are again. So tell me, what am I supposed to do? Turn myself into the police for a crime I didn't even commit?"

"You did commit a crime! You killed James!" Cassie gasped out her words as the gun continued to point in her direction. "You could have come forward with the truth about Mason. You would have done a little time as an accomplice, but you would have been free to go! Now, you're going to prison for murder!"

"Am I?" Jackson offered a menacing smile.

CHAPTER 29

Cassie met Tessa's eyes. She sensed the determination in the woman's gaze. It was two against one, and she guessed that Tessa had a plan to overpower Jackson. But she had no idea if it would work.

"Jackson, be reasonable here." Tessa frowned. "You're not going to be able to kill us both, and even if you do, it's not going to be easy to hide three bodies, now is it? That reporter you talked about, she's already on to you, and so is Ollie."

"Ollie is clueless." Jackson snorted. "I have him convinced that it was Zach."

"That's what you think, but it's not true." Cassie looked straight at him. "Ollie suspects you. He told me as much."

"Oh yeah? Then where is he?" Jackson glanced down the empty driveway. "We're all alone here, aren't we?"

"Not as alone as you think." Tessa squared her shoulders. "I called the police the moment Harry pulled that bone out from under the porch. I've kept the line open this whole time."

Cassie stared at her. She wanted to believe her, but she didn't. Something about the slight twang in her voice made her suspect that Tessa was trying to distract him. Which meant that she needed to take the opportunity for them to get away, if she could.

"Where's that phone?" Jackson barked at her as he walked toward her. "Give it to me right now!"

"Come Harry!" Cassie rushed up behind Jackson and clapped her hands.

Harry bolted toward her, which meant that his leash wrapped around the front of Jackson's legs.

As Jackson grabbed Tessa's purse, she yanked it backwards in the same moment that Cassie shoved him hard in the back.

Harry's leash caught Jackson by surprise. He tripped and fell toward Tessa.

"Tessa!" Cassie gasped as she saw the gun swing in her direction.

Tessa ducked out of Jackson's reach and in the same moment shoved his other arm and shoulder hard down to the ground.

For an instant, Cassie could see Tessa in full uniform, taking down a suspect, as if she had just walked out of training.

Cassie grabbed for the gun while Tessa wrestled with Jackson on the ground.

Flashing lights bathed them all in red and blue as a police car rushed down the driveway in their direction.

Startled, Cassie wondered if Tessa hadn't been bluffing at all.

With shaky hands she pointed the gun at Jackson. "Stay down, Jackson! It's over!"

Jackson froze at the sight of the gun in her hand.

Tessa pulled herself up to her feet and brushed the dirt from the knees of her pants.

"Well, it's about time, Ollie." She rolled her eyes as Oliver ran up to them with his gun aimed at Jackson.

Cassie held her breath as she lowered Jackson's gun. She could see the worry etched in every groove of Oliver's face. His grip on his weapon was so tight she wondered if he might actually pull the trigger.

Instead, he arrested Jackson. As he snapped the cuffs on him, he looked up at the two women.

"I'm sure there's going to be a thorough explanation for all of this."

"Absolutely." Tessa smiled. "Jackson will be happy to fill you in. Won't you, Jackson?" She tipped her head toward the porch. "You're going to need a forensic team out here. Mason Johnston is under that porch."

"I don't understand, didn't you hear everything on the phone, Ollie?" Cassie met his eyes.

"What?" Oliver stared back at her. "I ran into Sebastian and he asked me if I had seen you. I guess he has been trying to get a hold of you, and was concerned. I wonder why?" He raised an eyebrow. "Then when I was headed to Zach's house I saw your car here. I thought you might be here alone and I wanted to make sure you were okay. It seems like you put yourself in a very dangerous situation, yet again."

"Oh, drop it would you!" Tessa huffed. "The two of you would make an amazing investigative team if you would stop fighting with each other and work together!"

"The same could be said for the two of you." Cassie crossed her arms as she looked at Tessa. "I think it's time we all learned a little bit more about how to work together actually, and how to be grateful for each other."

"This is all very touching," Jackson muttered from the ground. "But if someone could get this dog to stop licking my face, I would really appreciate it."

"Harry!" Tessa guided him away from Jackson. "We don't lick the criminals, dear." She gave the dog a light pat on the top of the head. "Good boy by the way, very good boy."

Cassie had been in a similar situation with Tessa before, when Harry had helped catch two armed criminals. She knew that he was a very capable dog and presumed that it was too dangerous for Harry to try to restrain Jackson while he had the gun in his hand, otherwise Tessa would have instructed him to.

Oliver shook his head at both of them, then pulled Jackson to his feet.

"I'll need to speak with both of you about what happened here." Oliver's tone remained gruff as he guided Jackson to his car. "I need to process him first. Can we meet up tomorrow to go over all of this?"

"I'm busy tomorrow morning, but the afternoon would be perfect for me!" Cassie smiled. "We can all meet at my place. Alright Tessa?" She looked over at Tessa who only nodded.

"I'll be there. I want to hear every single word that led up to this." Oliver closed the back door of the car then turned to face Cassie. "Now, do you believe me when I tell you that you're putting yourself at risk?"

"Yes." Cassie recalled the sensation of the gun pressed against her back. "I believe you now, Ollie. I see how easily the most important people can be taken from us." Her heart softened as she noticed the sorrow that filled his eyes in reaction to her words. "We can talk about all of it tomorrow, alright?"

"I'll be there." Oliver nodded.

As Cassie and Tessa walked back to her car with Harry trotting along beside them, she noticed a scrape on Tessa's elbow.

"Tessa, you're hurt." Cassie reached out to touch it.

"I'm fine." Tessa tugged her sleeve down. "I'm proud of how quickly you picked up on my bluff, Cassie. I wasn't sure if you would."

"I wasn't sure if it was a bluff." Cassie started the car. "I'm just glad everything turned out alright. At least now James' murder is solved, and Mason's mother will get some closure. But this has been a very tough night."

"Yes, it has." Tessa stared out the window as they drove in the direction of home. "I think I could use a rest."

Harry barked from the back seat in agreement.

CHAPTER 30

"Watch it!" Sebastian ducked back as a cloud of flour puffed toward him.

"Sorry!" Cassie laughed as she watched the flour cling to his blond hair, nose, and cheeks.

"You don't sound sorry." Sebastian raised an eyebrow as he scooped up a handful of flour.

"No don't!" Cassie held up her hands. "There's so much to do! We have to hurry."

"This is a ridiculous plan, you know." Sebastian shook his head as he grabbed the apples out of the fridge and set them on the counter.

"I know, but it's the only one I have." Cassie peeked in the oven, then frowned. "I think it's almost done."

"That is the best turkey I've ever smelled." Sebastian poured the apples into the pie crust in front of him.

"Careful! We need to add some more spices to that." Cassie tasted the mixture then grabbed the spices from the counter and smiled as she added them. "I think I figured out Tessa's secret ingredient." She grinned as she held up a bottle of apple cider vinegar.

"I bet it will be delicious." Sebastian smiled.

Within minutes everyone would be arriving, and Cassie had no idea how they would react.

"I can't believe that you are the reason that Oliver showed up just in time last night. If you hadn't mentioned you couldn't find me he might have never stopped at the orchard when he saw my car." Cassie shook her head as she checked on the mashed potatoes and added a bit more salt.

"I thought you were upset with me when you didn't respond to my text, or my calls. I wanted to apologize. I just didn't know how, yet. I knew I should respect you not wanting to talk, but I wanted to make sure you were okay." Sebastian sighed. "I never should have walked away from you like I did. I was just frustrated. I felt like every word I said was giving you the wrong impression of me. It embarrassed me to think that you thought I agreed with the way Zach acted when he was drunk. Then, I wondered if maybe you were better off listening to Ollie instead of me." He frowned. "I just needed a minute to figure it all out, I was pretty confused."

"I think you had pretty good reason to be." Cassie frowned as she turned to face him. "I've been sending you some very mixed signals, and you've been quite clear with me."

"I've tried to be." Sebastian gazed at her. "But maybe I shouldn't have pushed so hard."

"If the invitation for the concert still stands, I'd like to take you up on it." Cassie's heart raced as she spoke those words.

"It absolutely stands." Sebastian reached for her hand. "I'd be happy to spend the time with you."

Cassie curled her fingers around his and smiled. As he leaned toward her, a bit of flour drifted off of his hair and settled on her cheek. Just before his lips would have touched hers, someone knocked on the front door.

"Oh!" Cassie gasped as she took a step back from him. "This is it!"

"Cassie, no matter what happens, I've got your

back." Sebastian smiled as he looked toward the door. "But be prepared for a very rough ride."

Cassie walked up to the front door and pulled it open. Outside, Oliver stood in a business suit with his gun belt around his waist. He was clearly still working and expected to just be there to take their statements.

"What smells so good?" Oliver sniffed the air and peered past her.

"Come in and find out." Cassie smiled as she waved to Tessa, who walked up onto the porch behind him with Harry close behind. "Just in time, Tessa!"

"What's going on here?" Tessa scowled, as she followed Cassie into the kitchen.

"I just have to get the turkey out, and we'll be ready to eat!" Cassie clapped her hands.

Harry ran over to be petted by Sebastian.

"Cassie!" Tessa's voice cracked as sharply as a whip as she looked around at the biscuits, potatoes, vegetables, and the pie waiting to go in the oven. "What have you done?"

Cassie turned to face Tessa and Oliver, and took a deep breath. "I know about Alice." She held up her hands. "I know that you both lost someone who was incredibly special to both of you." She looked between the two of them. "Tessa, you lost a close friend." She looked back at Oliver. "And you lost your mother, probably before you had the chance to really get to know her."

"Cassie." Oliver rubbed his hand along the back of his neck. "I'm just here to take a statement, that's all."

"No, that's not all, Ollie." Cassie took his hand, then took Tessa's. "Before I came here, I had no one. I lost the only family I had left, and really, we weren't very close. I know what it's like to be alone. But now, I know what it's like to be surrounded by people who care about me, who want to make sure that I'm safe, and who will put up with my curious side." She glanced over at Sebastian as she smiled, then looked back at Tessa and Oliver. "Some people say we don't get to choose our family, and that's true. But it's true not just of our blood families. Just because you might not see eye to eye on things, that doesn't make you any less family. Tessa loved your mother as a sister, Ollie, and she loves you, too. Ollie, I know that you adore Tessa, and all of this silliness of being apart, it's going to stop today."

Harry barked playfully as if he wanted everyone's attention. Sebastian crouched down and rubbed behind his ears.

"Just because you say so?" Tessa frowned. "That's not how life works, Cassie."

"No, but that's how families work. You can still be angry at each other, if you feel you need to, but you can't deny that you're family. I'd like to think we all are. Or at least we're the closest thing we've got to it." Cassie squeezed Oliver's hand. "Maybe life hasn't treated any of us the way we expected, but it brought us all here, to this moment, to share a delicious meal together, and remember how it feels to be surrounded by people who care about us."

"Cassie, this isn't going to work." Oliver pulled his hand from hers. "I can't go through what I went through with my mother again. I can't be close to someone, to Tessa, and lose them."

"Lose me?" Tessa frowned. "What are you talking about, Ollie? You aren't going to lose me."

"When we were on that job together." Oliver's voice wavered. "The one where you got shot. You could have been killed because you were trying to protect me. I thought I was going to lose you because you put yourself in a dangerous situation because of me. So, I cut myself off from you. Just like I did from my mother. She must have been so angry with me."

"Why would you think she was angry with you?"

Tessa tried to catch his eyes which were looking at the floor.

"For walking away from her, the same way my father did. When she got sick I panicked and I went to live with my father instead of staying with her. She said it was okay, but how could I abandon her like that. I should have stayed with her. I just couldn't deal with it. I thought, there would always be time." Oliver frowned. "She must have hated me for it."

"Never." Tessa looked into his eyes. "Never once did your mother feel anything but love and pride for you, Ollie. You were a kid. She wanted you to live with your father. She wanted you to be protected. She didn't want you to know how sick she was. She didn't want you to be caught up in taking care of her. When I left Little Leaf Creek after your mother passed away, I knew your father would take care of you and you could move forward with your life. I thought you were angry with me because I didn't follow orders and that was why I was shot, not because you thought I got shot because of you."

"Angry at you?" Oliver shook his head as he gazed into her eyes. "How could I be angry at you for protecting me, for probably saving my life. For being there for my mother, for holding her hand through it all. I have no idea how I can ever tell you how grateful I am for that. When I saw you get shot I panicked, I thought I was going to lose you, too, so I distanced myself from you. I tried to protect myself."

"Let's start again?" Tessa took his hand.

"Yes, let's start again." Oliver smiled slightly.

"See?" Cassie smiled as she watched the two of them hug. "Maybe I never had the chance to meet Alice, but I know in my heart that this is exactly what she would have wanted."

"Cassie." Tessa pulled away from Oliver as she quickly wiped a tear from her eye. "I think something is burning."

"Oh no!" Cassie gasped as she turned toward the oven. "Not the turkey!"

"I'll get it!" Sebastian pulled open the oven, which caused smoke to billow out into the kitchen.

"Maybe it's not the right day, but now it's definitely Thanksgiving!" Cassie laughed.

"I'm sure it will taste great." Sebastian pulled her gently into his arms and placed a light kiss on her cheek.

Cassie felt a rush of sparks as his lips grazed her skin, and for an instant she could picture every Thanksgiving exactly the same way. She pushed the thought away and smiled at him. She didn't need to overthink it. She just needed to enjoy the wonderful day. She couldn't wait to see what the future held for her in Little Leaf Creek. She imagined a very eventful Christmas was on the way.

The End

LITTLE LEAF CREEK COZY MYSTERY SERIES

Chaos in Little Leaf Creek

Peril in Little Leaf Creek

CHOCOLATE CENTERED COZY MYSTERIES

The Sweet Smell of Murder

A Deadly Delicious Delivery

A Bitter Sweet Murder

A Treacherous Tasty Trail

Pastry and Peril

Trouble and Treats

Fudge Films and Felonies

Custom-Made Murder

Skydiving, Soufflés and Sabotage

Christmas Chocolates and Crimes

Hot Chocolate and Homicide

Chocolate Caramels and Conmen

<u>Picnics, Pies and Lies</u>

<u>Devils Food Cake and Drama</u>

<u>Cinnamon and a Corpse</u>

<u>Cherries, Berries and a Body</u>

<u>Christmas Cookies and Criminals</u>

<u>Grapes, Ganache & Guilt</u>

DUNE HOUSE COZY MYSTERIES

<u>Seaside Secrets</u>

<u>Boats and Bad Guys</u>

<u>Treasured History</u>

<u>Hidden Hideaways</u>

<u>Dodgy Dealings</u>

<u>Suspects and Surprises</u>

<u>Ruffled Feathers</u>

<u>A Fishy Discovery</u>

<u>Danger in the Depths</u>

<u>Celebrities and Chaos</u>

<u>Pups, Pilots and Peril</u>

<u>Tides, Trails and Trouble</u>

<u>Racing and Robberies</u>

<u>Athletes and Alibis</u>

Birthdays Can Be Deadly

Money Can Be Deadly

Trust Can Be Deadly

Ties Can Be Deadly

Rocks Can Be Deadly

Jewelry Can Be Deadly

Numbers Can Be Deadly

Memories Can Be Deadly

Paintings Can Be Deadly

Snow Can Be Deadly

Tea Can Be Deadly

Greed Can Be Deadly

Clutter Can Be Deadly

NUTS ABOUT NUTS COZY MYSTERIES

A Tough Case to Crack

A Seed of Doubt

Roasted Peanuts and Peril

Chestnuts, Camping and Culprits

DONUT TRUCK COZY MYSTERIES

Deadly Deals and Donuts

Fatal Festive Donuts

Bunny Donuts and a Body

Strawberry Donuts and Scandal

Frosted Donuts and Fatal Falls

BEKKI THE BEAUTICIAN COZY MYSTERIES

Hairspray and Homicide

A Dyed Blonde and a Dead Body

Mascara and Murder

Pageant and Poison

Conditioner and a Corpse

Mistletoe, Makeup and Murder

Hairpin, Hair Dryer and Homicide

Blush, a Bride and a Body

Shampoo and a Stiff

Cosmetics, a Cruise and a Killer

Lipstick, a Long Iron and Lifeless

Camping, Concealer and Criminals

Treated and Dyed

WENDY THE WEDDING PLANNER COZY
MYSTERIES

ABOUT THE AUTHOR

Cindy Bell is a USA Today and Wall Street Journal Bestselling Author. She is the author of the Little Leaf Creek, Wagging Tail, Donut Truck, Dune House, Sage Gardens, Chocolate Centered, Macaron Patisserie, Nuts about Nuts, Bekki the Beautician, Heavenly Highland Inn and Wendy the Wedding Planner cozy mystery series.

Cindy has always loved reading, but it is only recently that she has discovered her passion for writing romantic cozy mysteries. She loves walking along the beach thinking of the next adventure her characters can embark on.

You can sign up for her newsletter so you are notified of her latest releases at http://www.cindybellbooks.com.

Ingredients:

Pie Crust

2 1/2 cups all-purpose flour, plus more for dusting
1 teaspoon ground cinnamon
1/2 teaspoon salt
2 tablespoons granulated sugar
1 cup (8 ounces) very cold unsalted butter cut into cubes
4 to 8 tablespoons ice cold water

1 egg lightly beaten for brushing the pastry

Filling

2 1/2 pounds slightly tart apples
2/3 cup light brown sugar
2 teaspoons ground cinnamon
1/2 teaspoon ground allspice
1/2 teaspoon ground nutmeg
3 tablespoons butter
2 tablespoons apple cider vinegar
2 tablespoons cornstarch

Preparation:

For the pie crust, mix the flour, cinnamon, salt and sugar in a bowl.

Using your fingertips, rub in the cold cubed butter until the mixture resembles fine breadcrumbs.

Gradually add the water until the dough can be formed into a ball. Make sure the dough does not become too wet.

Divide into two portions and shape them into disks. One portion should be about two thirds of the dough which is used for the bottom and sides of the pie. The other third is for the lattice top.

Cover the dough with plastic wrap and refrigerate for at least one hour.

To make the filling peel, core and cut the apples into about 3/4-inch slices and place in a bowl.

Mix in the sugar, cinnamon, allspice. and nutmeg.

In a large saucepan over medium heat melt the butter.

Add the apple mixture to the melted butter.

Cook for about 4 minutes, stirring occasionally.

Add the apple cider vinegar and cornstarch to the apple mixture. Mix together and cook for another 2 to 4 minutes, stirring occasionally. The apples should be just slightly soft as they will continue to cook in the pie.

You only want enough of the thick liquid remaining to coat the apples.

Place the mixture in a bowl and leave aside to cool. You can have a taste and add more spices if desired.

Once completely cooled the filling can be used straight away or left covered in the fridge overnight.

When you are ready to bake the pie, remove the dough from the fridge.

If the pastry is too hard to roll leave it at room temperature for 5 to 10 minutes.

Preheat the oven to 350 degrees Fahrenheit.

On a lightly floured surface roll out the larger portion of the dough and use it to line the bottom and sides of a 9-inch diameter glass pie pan. Trim the sides.

Place parchment paper and rice or baking beads over the top of the crust.

Bake the crust in the oven for 10 minutes.

To make the lattice top, roll out the other portion of the pastry to the same diameter to fit the top of the pie. Cut into 1-inch strips.

Stir the cooled apple mixture and then pour it into the pastry case.

Take the strips of pastry and carefully weave them to form a lattice on the top of the pie. Cut the edges so it is in line with the pie dish.

Brush the lightly beaten egg over the pastry using a pastry brush.

Place the pie in the oven and bake for 30 to 40 minutes, until the pastry is golden and cooked through.

Serve hot or cold with ice cream or cream.

Enjoy!!

www.ingramcontent.com/pod-product-compliance
Lightning Source LLC
Chambersburg PA
CBHW072215150726
48002CB00005B/1818